# Frozen Brazilian Delight

## The Frozen Brazilian Series
### Book 1

CeCe Rubin

# Contents


1. Delight — 1
2. Buy A Car, Win A Friend — 12
3. Redemption And Broken Homes — 18
4. Driving Level Expert — 24
5. Laws, Not Suggestions — 30
6. Jerry Springer And The Chili Show — 36
7. Sheets — 43
8. The Place I Don't Belong — 47
9. The Ranch — 53
10. The Gray Dog — 62
11. Ohio Samba — 66
12. Love In The Listing Ship — 72
13. Sorry, Ma'am, We Had To Deploy An Aircraft… — 77
14. Lawn And Order — 84
15. Overalls In Tall Grass — 91
16. Scorpion's March — 98
17. The Goblin — 105
18. Duty And The Ties That Bind — 111
19. The Clergyman — 119
20. The Exit Flu — 130

About the Author — 145

# Chapter 1

## *Delight*

G rowing up in the sweltering heat in my home in Brazil, I dreamt of the snowy mountains depicted in one of my favorite movies, *The Sound of Music*. I would run and twirl with my arms outstretched, my head facing the sky as I belted my version of the "The hills are alive" song, rolling my tongue in what I believe to be English.

I would twirl and sing for two minutes under the hot January sun before collapsing on the grass breathless, looking for any vestige of water molecules leftover from the morning dew.

My face rested on the cool grass, giving me some relief as the sweat poured down my face. As I lay in the grass, I would summon the image of the snow-capped mountains in the Swiss Alps, seen in the background where Maria, the lucky nun, got to run and play.

My mother would see me on the grass through the open windows of our first-floor apartment; she would yell for me to get up "this instant" in her exasperated tone of voice, mostly used when she addressed her youngest and "wildest" child.

I would then get up and slowly make my way up to our first-floor apartment, using the elevator to avoid any more physical strain. I would imagine myself as a nun, even though I wasn't sure of Jewish nuns living in convents, certainly not in Brazil, where the heat would have made wearing a full habit very uncomfortable.

My parents, who had immigrated from Poland to Israel and later Brazil, never thought of installing air conditioning; they enjoyed "the warmth," as they used to call it. The heat relieved them from the memories of the relentless cold in Poland as they tried to survive The Second World War and the concentration camps. They would smile in delight at my reddened sweaty face, and, in their childhood dialect, they would say to me, "Ah Mehaie," what a delightful life.

Seeing their smiling faces through my sweaty bangs, I would try to match their joy. I would say, "Yes, absolutely," while gulping huge quantities of Hawaiian Punch. I was determined to deliver hydration to my brain to plot my escape from the humid tropical heat the moment I turned 18.

"If I make it," I would grumble, lying down by the opened window, waiting for the "cool breeze" my parents swore they felt in the constant 90-degree weather.

My parents worked together all day long; my siblings, much older than me, busied themselves all day with their studies and romantic pursuits.

That left me with hours of solitude with the opportunity to explore the world around me; Geralda, the live-in maid, was my constant companion. My exploits frazzled her nerves. She would reluctantly agree to sit on the sofa and watch my latest theater performance, which was preferable to her than having to look for me as I disappeared into the building complex, looking for adventures, tired of watching cartoons and Zorro. Geralda would invariably fall asleep, her mouth open, apparently unmoved by my carefully choreographed versions of the American musicals I would watch on tv.

Geralda's naps during my "shows" ended one day after she found herself with a mouth filled with the peanuts that I had carefully placed in her open mouth, thinking that she most likely was falling asleep due to lacking enough nutrition.

Geralda gasped, spitting out the peanuts and her set of dentures that landed on the sofa next to her. I looked at Geralda's teeth, horrified by my first experience of seeing false teeth. Geralda quickly retrieved her teeth and left me alone as she walked into the bathroom, closing her door.

Seeing the scattered peanuts led me to check my teeth, fully expecting to be able to remove them, gums and all. I found my teeth to be entirely secure to my gums. For several days after that experience, I would slowly chew my food while intermittently checking that my teeth were still in place until my mother told me to "cut it out."

Food was abundant in my childhood home due to my parents' trauma of hunger and starvation during their time spent in the concentration camps in Poland and Germany. My parents kept themselves trim and fit. They ate without excess, offering their children, Geralda, and anyone who crossed the threshold of our home beautifully arranged platters of food. My parents would eat a small amount while encouraging others to eat, their eyes slanting as they smiled, happy with their ability to feed others.

Geralda's loyalty toward me kept her silent about my latest exploits.

I was lonely, bored, and curious. I would walk around the apartment checking my mother's trinkets. I soon became fascinated by the clocks of all sizes we had all over our house. I had no idea of the clock's utility at that age. Despite my young age, I would feel a twinge of guilt as I plotted to take the table clock apart. Still, my intense curiosity had me sneaking kitchen utensils to my room, where I would dismantle the clocks, piece by piece, looking for the source of the ticking sound and watching the moving parts, fascinated by the mechanical magic.

Once the sound and movement ceased, and the pile of gears and screws lay on my bed, I would start the reassembling attempt; inexplicably, there were always some leftover pieces that would not fit. I would tell myself that such tiny pieces couldn't possibly cause the clock's mechanism to fail. But they all did, falling silent, the hands immobile as it showed the exact moment I had initiated my exploration.

The mystery of the clock's loss of functionality joined the other mysterious occurrences in my home, including the missing Mercury from the glass thermometer. I would break the thermometer, collecting the silvery Mercury in my hands before transferring it into an empty matchbox. I entertained myself for hours, fascinated by the silvery Mercury's ability to divide itself into smaller sizes at the touch of my finger; I would run Mercury races inside the bottom portion of the matchbox. I would pretend that the shiny droplets were little bugs racing each other to the finish line I drew with my Bic pen. I lifted one side of the box slowly, creating an incline that would cause the silver droplets to tumble down to the "finish line." My parents never found out about my "Mercury pet" collection. I always wondered if handling the deadly chemical with my bare hands and storing it in an empty box with phosphorus residue contributed to my fertile imagination and short attention span.

One day during Carnaval, my mother returned home early from work, tired and nursing a nasty migraine. She found me wearing the living room curtains, the silky fabric carefully arranged around my body, secured by pins to one side of the shoulder. I saw her and raised my arm, holding a flashlight. I hoped to show her my best Statue of Liberty impression; I had decided on that custom for the Carnaval celebration in our club that evening. My mother stared at me, apparently at a loss for words, which was a rarity for her.

That was the day my enrollment in the all-day Summer camp during vacation and after school. My parents had decided for my sake, for the integrity of the house furnishings, and for my safety.

My afternoons were now busy with ballet, piano, and art

classes. A tutor helped me with my homework even though I completed my assignments without his help. The tutor, a quiet and shy Math teacher, made extra money by keeping myself and the home in one piece while my parents worked.

He was kind and appeared to be thoroughly amused by my keen interest in science and my preference for Classical music due to watching *Looney Tunes*. He took me to museums and landmarks around São Paulo, my town. One day he arrived with tickets for a Classical concert that night at the beautiful "Teatro Municipal" in the town center. He was sure he had a child prodigy in his hands as he led me to our Burgundy velour seats close to the orchestra. I arranged my favorite organza dress around me, and, pulling my socks up, I spent a minute admiring the sheen of my patent leather shoes. That was the last thing I remember as minutes into Beethoven's 5th Symphony for piano and orchestra; I fell asleep.

São Paulo is an 18 million-people behemoth of a town, where the skyscrapers compete for space in the skies that are frequently grey, the sun peeking through the heavy smog and pollution. Not exactly the mental image you would conjure up when thinking about Brazil. The tropical paradise with gorgeous beaches and scantily clad people, laying in the scorching sun, bodies glistening with sweat and homemade tanner, a mixture of Coca-Cola and baby oil.

The lush forests shown on *National Geographic* specials, where monkeys jump from tree to tree, the forest teeming with life and sound is the Brazil of people's imagination. Those lucky enough to leave São Paulo and Rio de Janeiro for the beautiful small towns and villages lining the coast, all the way to the Amazon forest, would see the lush generations, blue skies, and miles and miles of fine white sands and blue-green ocean water. The trees in São Paulo grew restricted in small parks where the only wild things to be found were stray cats and the occasional drunk, sleeping off the party from the night before. I lived in one of those skyscrapers; our apartment was on the first floor, and there were 27 more floors, with two apartments on each floor above our unit. Two elevators whizzed up and down, carrying the residents all day long. I sometimes rode in the elevator before my "tutor's" arrival. I was curious about the lives of those who lived above me. I would get off on a random floor, inspecting my neighbor's choices for decorating their hallway between apartment "A" on the right and "B" on the left.

I would imagine their day-to-day lives behind closed doors until I heard approaching steps at their front door. I quickly used the stairs to evade detection, listening to their goodbyes, "Tchau, see you later!" to the other people inside as I silently walked down to the next floor. I would think about the families that resided in our building, "Would their lives be much different than mine"?

As a budding social scientist, I wondered about humans and their habits.

My parents had immigrated from Israel to Brazil looking for warmth and peace as they tried to leave behind Poland, the concentration camps, and the Second World War. They had spent seven years in Israel right after the war. They fought in Israel's Independence War, and soon after, they left for Brazil, where a distant cousin, also a survivor, lived. The cousin invited my parents to her new home country—my parents left for Brazil in an old ocean liner; they had a total of thirty-five dollars to their names and two little kids, my sister and my brother.

Brazil, with its warm climate and slow pace where everyone had time for a chat and "cafezinho," the strong expresso served in tiny cups all day and night, was like a salve on my parents' many wounds.

They never installed air conditioning, as the chill of the nights spent in the concentration camp barracks would creep back into their memories when they had "bad days." We had small fans in a closet for the "real hot nights." In Brazil, the median temperature was in the high eighties day or night. During June and July, Brazil's short Winter season, the temperature fluctuated in the 70s and upper 60s; anything below that would be considered a national emergency. Brazilians would have canceled their plans to stay home bundled up in wool blankets near their electric heater, hoping the cooler temperatures were not a sign of the world's end.

My parents quickly immersed themselves in the culture, befriending the easygoing Brazilians; their Polish accents became barely noticeable after a while, and they had full command of the Portuguese language. They loved the warm climate and the warmth of the Brazilians.

They admired the importance of social connections in Brazilian culture. A Brazilian would gladly interrupt an important meeting or errand to offer a helping hand or to engage in a quick chat, offering the obligatory "cafezinho" and a bite of "pao de queijo," a delicious cheesy bread made with Cassava flour and parmesan cheese, lots of it.

A good-natured chat with relatives, friends, and strangers is often seen as a unique opportunity to potentially meet your "best friends for life," as long as the stranger isn't a smiling robber or pickpocket.

Brazilians have always been enthusiastic in their greetings to each other. The "oi" or "oiiii" salute is delivered with a broad smile, full eye contact, and two kisses, one on each cheek.

Friendliness is expected in all encounters, creating opportunities for easy laughter and connection. My parents and siblings, born 18 months apart in Israel, thrived in Brazil.

My sister was thirteen, my brother was twelve when I made my presence known to my mother, who had thought for months that she was experiencing early menopause until she felt my first movements in her womb.

At that point in their lives, my parents led busy work and social lives. They were intensely committed to charity work geared towards social justice and culture. Finally, my mother felt my first movements consistently enough to consider her belly sensations may be something other than gas. She described her symptoms to the doctor and asked him about the possibility that early menopause and a case of food poisoning could be the reason for her symptoms. The doctor confirmed she would have a "pause" for about five months until my delivery. I made my arrival into this world in January 1962.

I was happy and easygoing as a baby; my parents were delighted with the chance to experience parenthood in a time of peace and stability. Life continued at the usual pace. My mother returned to work with my father. They hired Dona Olga, a sweet elderly lady that became my second mom.

Despite the oppressive heat, I made it to my 18th birthday, and by 27, I had run out of excuses regarding finding a mate.

I married my first husband, whom I met on a blind date arranged by my father and the chief rabbi in our congregation. The matter regarding finding me a husband was now at the hands of the famous long-haired American rabbi of the biggest Temple in São Paulo.

My ex and I met at the restaurant of the highest building in my town. The tall windows surrounded the dinners, offering a breathtaking view of the city; looking at things from a great distance can, at times, trick the eyes into seeing beauty. At close inspection, however, the gritty nature of life in the concrete jungle is exposed.

My ex met me at the restaurant; I recognized him from our temple; he was glowing from a bad case of sunburn that his turquoise short-sleeve shirt made even more pronounced, as well as the white slacks and the white suspenders that completed his outfit.

After a year of courtship, we married and moved to Cincinnati, "Ohaio." I later learned that the correct spelling was Ohio, pronounced as "Ohaio", which made no sense to me.

I thought about my opinion shared by all Brazilians regarding all things American. All Americans are brilliant; a lesson learned by growing up watching American movies dubbed into Portuguese, witnessing the moon landing, and crying in despair when the greatest president to rule a nation, President Kennedy, was assassinated. Americans had gone to the moon and created Hollywood and Coca-Cola; they could have made spoken English as it's written or vice versa.

We arrived in Cincinnati in late October, and the houses clad in Halloween decorations lined the streets. We were in awe and somewhat terrified seeing the ghoulish decor that depicted cemetery scenes at people's front doors!

My Brazilian/Jewish superstition-laden upbringing caused me to shiver in horror. I laughed nervously at the sight of the ghoulish decorations, scaring myself with my laugh. I tried to appear calm and casual about the scene. I knew that my then-husband would have shown minimal sympathy for my fears. My future ex seemed unperturbed by the witches on brooms and skeletons hanging from the trees. He had been raised in a secular Jewish home in Argentina by Argentinian-born parents, where nothing scary ever happened other than Evita Peron becoming president.

My ex drove us to our first American motel, talking excitedly about the "smooth ride" as he drove his first automatic transmission car. I would nod and smile, looking at him with the bright-eyed attention of a newlywed. I would turn my attention to the dismal scenes as my ex would pause to take a long drag from his cigarette. The nine hours spent on the plane had prevented him from enjoying his habit of inhaling big puffs of nicotine, a habit that never made sense to me. Oxygen was free and readily available; purposely inhaling air pollutants seemed foolish to me.

The car rental hummed quietly; the smooth asphalt of the well-kept roads and the car's great suspension made me sleepy. My last conscious thought before falling asleep was about hope; I hoped that our arrival in America during Halloween would not be foretelling a grim future in our new home. Thinking back, I must have experienced insight regarding the future demise of my first marriage.

I jumped headfirst into the American language and culture.

The supermarket tabloids helped me learn English. I remembered "needing" desperately to learn the fate of the alien baby found in a field in Minnesota and other such fantastic news. Johnny Carson would become instrumental in my acquisition of the English language, I would hear how the audience laughed at his stories, and I wanted to laugh with them.

My introduction to American cuisine was fascinating. My first meal consisted of a pile of crumbly meat in an oily colorless sauce that spilled from under the spaghetti that made its base. The server said that the dish was a "Cincinnati delicacy." I approached the task of tasting the food with the same enthusiasm I had for everything American. I chewed and swallowed the gray-brown meat and retreated to my internal dialogue, where I tried to convince myself that this dish was a gastronomic miracle.

The Cincinnati Chili saga is described later in this tale of adventure and regret for assuming that "everything" in America would always be of my liking. The dessert, two slices of apple pie "a la mode," arrived with another American delicacy only available during Halloween, according to our server. The pretty yellow and orange pyramid-shaped candy was set on the table in a little bowl and placed next to the pies. I reached for the sweets, my mouth eagerly anticipating the deliciousness of a piece of candy corn.

The problem must have been my expectations. I stopped chewing the candy, my brain attempting to locate a similar taste in my memory bank. The taste and texture confused me; the words "candy" and "corn" did not belong together. It was just "so wrong," I thought to myself. I looked at my ex as he chewed handfuls of the candy; his taste buds must have lost their ability to discern yummy from weird, most likely due to his cigarette smoking. I gave him a sympathetic look as I discreetly spat the offending candy on a paper napkin, finally relieving my mouth from the weird taste.

Great expectations can be a source of heartache, as it was in this case. The taste of my first American treat, which I had hoped would blow my mind, did, but not in a good way. I tried to regain my enthusiasm but could only feel doubt creeping in as I started to fear that this first disappointment for an American original would spell trouble for my desire to one day join this exceptional nation as one of their own. I let out a sigh, piercing the flaky crust of the apple pie with the fork and dipping it in the rapidly melting vanilla ice cream on my plate. As I placed it in my mouth, all of my doubts and fears disappeared; I finished the apple pie, scraping the plate, looking for any remaining morsel of the American pie. I knew then that my dream of being an American would come true. I leaned back in my seat, feeling satisfied and nurtured; the feeling brought back my and my parents' words to me, "h Mehaie," I whispered to myself; what a wonderful delight.

# Chapter 2

---

## *Buy A Car, Win A Friend*

B ack in Cincinnati, where my first experience in America started, I was enthralled by what I thought to be the fantastic American ingenuity and its greatness as a nation.

My ex and I exited the car dealership driving our first automatic car. We moved slowly, my ex at the wheel. We shared our thoughts regarding our first experience at an American car dealership. We were thoroughly impressed by the attentiveness of the car salesman, whom we felt was now our friend for life.

The car salesman appeared to be deeply concerned about our safety. We were touched by how caring he was as he suggested or, better yet, insisted that we purchase all the extra safety features for our new vehicle, telling us that our new car would be almost indestructible. We signed the contract with all the options suggested to us. As we finished signing the paperwork, we noticed the other car sales associates standing by us, smiling and nodding in approval. Soon, the dealership manager came by the desk where we sat and congratulated us on our astute purchase. We felt touched by their enthusiasm over our acquisition of a night-blue Pontiac Grand Prix, automatic with six cylinders with all the options and the newest features.

We received the paperwork handed to us and a faux leather case. We placed it in the glove compartment. We had agreed before buying the car that only an American-made vehicle would do. We wanted to honor our new country by supporting their industry!

We had shown patriotic disdain for all foreign-made automobiles during our few outings to look for a vehicle before deciding that becoming an American meant appreciating and supporting manufacturers of America the great.

We had to trade our international driver's license for an Ohio one. We drove home excited about our upcoming experience at the local Bureau of Motor Vehicles the next day. We would soon complete our metamorphosis, shedding our out-of-towers status to become Cincinnati residents with a document to prove it!

That night we barely slept. We spent some time trying to make sense of the documents we had just signed to purchase the Pontiac. We soon gave up, concentrating instead on planning a Brazilian barbecue where we would invite our new friend, the car salesman, and maybe the dealership's manager to show them our appreciation for their care and attention. We felt that those kind individuals were our first American friends. After discussing the barbecue menu, we returned our attention to the mind-numbing task of understanding the sales and purchase contract and the other documents to know what to bring to the BMV the next day.

I would search through the English-Spanish Thesaurus for the words my ex wanted to translate. I believe I fell asleep first, lulled to sleep by my ex's strong Argentinian accent, waking up startled by him shouting triumphantly, "car haff varanti!" That must have been all he needed to know since he collapsed into the pillow, happy that our new car had a warranty. He was soon fast asleep.

The next day bright and early, we ate a hearty breakfast at Denny's. My ex proclaimed that the meal confirmed America's excellence in everything as he filled his mouth with hash browns, steak, and eggs.

My opinion on the steak that I eyed suspiciously was that it looked a bit pale with a slight green tinge at its sides. I ate a bite of my pancakes arranged in a high pile, drenched in butter and maple syrup. We marveled at the portion sizes as we watched the lovely server transfer the remaining food in two styrofoam containers that we carried back to the car in plastic bags.

We left Denny's pretty content with enough food to last us for two days. We sat down on our Pontiac Grand Prix, feeling full and a bit nauseous. Despite our shared symptoms of gastric distress, we left for the BMV, my ex at the wheel and me looking blankly at the map I was expected to read and give my ex the exact coordinates to the Cincinnati BMV. We drove for about an hour. The first 40 minutes we spent backing up, making U-turns, and finally stopped at a Kroger's supermarket for directions and Tums. We arrived at the BMV feeling free of our gastric distress.

We drove utterly silent, popping Tums in our mouths until we felt better. We could now speak to each other without risking letting out a burp. I confessed to my ex that I was "map illiterate."

The directions I had given him were based on gut feeling and instinct; in fairness, my gut feelings are usually right unless I am experiencing dyspepsia, which I was before eating Tums.

We walked into a brightly lit space. People were standing in a line that led to a window where a person would listen to their request and then hand them a tiny piece of paper with a number written on it. We got our numbers, and the attendant directed us to a bookshelf where we could select the necessary forms. The shelf had English and Spanish forms and all the languages you would expect to find in the United Nations. My ex and I smiled at each other; we agreed that we were witnessing another sign of America's commitment to making all immigrants feel included, even at the BMV.

We were so eager to be part of this great nation! We boldly

reached for the forms in English. We walked proudly to the back of the room where rows and rows of people sat in chairs, all holding the little piece of paper as they stared at an electronic panel that periodically lit up with a number. A disembodied female voice would then announce, "Now serving number x at the x window."

We sat with our respective forms attached to a clipboard with a pen secured by a plastic string.

We proceeded to exchange our perspectives on the content of the forms. We were in trouble, and we knew it. We should have used forms in Spanish. We had grossly overestimated our fluency in English. I suggested we go home and retrieve the dictionary English- Spanish and bring it back to the BMV.

We felt ashamed that the "English in a week" course we took back home failed to give the promised results. My ex wouldn't budge. He glared at me and used his index finger to make several circular motions in rapid succession by his temple, communicating his feelings about my suggestions to bring the dictionary to the BMV or to take the forms home and use the dictionary at home. Spanish is an emphatic language requiring the speaker to use as many hand gestures as possible.

I learned Spanish from my ex during our year of courtship. I joined him in the animated discussion using my Portuguese hand gestures. I continued to defend my point that under-standing the form was far more important than pride or shame, and it would give us a better chance to obtain the much-desired American driver's license.

At some point in our interchange, we realized that the room was falling silent; feeling watched, we looked around the room, meeting the gaze of the people around us.

A mother held her baby's bottle in the air, distracted by our argument that may have sounded like an episode of *I Love Lucy*

The baby in the stroller craned his neck, attempting to reach the bottle held by his mother, still suspended in mid-air. We immediately stopped arguing and greeted our small audience with "hello" and "very good, ok?" Smiling and giving the thumbs-up sign.

I got up and walked to the shelves, placing the slightly crumpled forms on the shelf marked "English." I collected the papers from the frame labeled "Spanish," returning to my seat next to my ex. We quickly completed the forms and watched the electronic board for our number.

We looked around the room, noticing that we seemed to be one of the few foreign nationals. Our brightly colored shirts depicting coconut trees and pineapples were a dead giveaway of our provenance, very noticeable in a sea of jeans and flannel shirts in discrete dark blue and maroon colors.

We decided to go shopping for clothing with less Carmen Miranda flavor for more John Wayne clothes as soon as possible.

Finally, we heard our number call; we approached the window, smiling brightly, ready to make another friend in America, just like our first friend, the car salesman. The man at the window stared at us blankly; he took the forms from us and quickly started to stamp and sort the papers at a dizzying speed. He made periodic clicking sounds with his mouth, which caused me to make a couple of clicking sounds of my own due to an undiagnosed ADD condition at that time.

My ex glared at me and hissed, "Que te passa?" which brought my clicking sounds to an end. The man at the window appeared unaware of my sudden acquisition of his tics; he left momentarily and returned with two small books he handed us. He spoke with a deep drawl, but we understood the words "study guide" and "exam." He pointed to the calendar with a date for a week from that day when we would return to take "the exam."

The man seemed to have instructed individuals who had spoken and understood little English. He pretended to write in the air and said, "Exam." We nodded enthusiastically at the hand-communication abilities shown by this man. He then pretended to be holding onto a steering wheel, turning the imaginary car from left to right, and repeating the word "exam." We again nodded while we gave the man on the window our driving-in-the-air interpretation. I even pretended to use the horn to communicate our understanding of his gestures until I noticed my ex's Ricky Ricardo expression returning to his face. We thanked the man profusely. We left the BMV building holding our study guides and with our renewed hope for a bright future as drivers in America.

# Chapter 3

## *Redemption And Broken Homes*

O n our way home, we stopped at Kroger's, the supermarket we had briefly visited on our way to the BMV to buy Tums. We needed food and other supplies. Our refrigerator was so empty that anything placed in it would produce an echo.

Our first apartment in America was a ground floor "garden-style" unit in a student housing complex, within walking distance to the University where my ex planned to complete his Master's degree.

On our way to Kroger's entrance, we saw a sign that read "Redemption Center." We walked into the supermarket, discussing the sign we had just read. We assumed that sign was a concrete example of American generosity and faith. Americans shop for their groceries, and they stop at the "Redemption Center" on their way out to redeem themselves and help the community simultaneously. We were humbled and happy to have found ourselves among such excellent and caring people.

Inside the supermarket, we saw rows of shelves in each aisle crammed with various brands of the same product.

In a Brazilian or Argentinian supermarket, we would find three or, at most, four brands; we were stunned and confused. We walked the aisles with our empty cart, unsure of what product to pick. My ex decided that we should start shopping for fresh produce where we could recognize the variety displayed in neat piles. The dizzying array of products kicked on my ADD, which was still undiagnosed.

My ex moved quickly, pushing the cart towards an apple pyramid; I had found the candy aisle and stood there, transfixed by the colors and sweet smells. My ex found me holding several bags of delicious candy. I laughed nervously, arranging the bags in my arms to prevent them from sliding to the ground. My ex gave me "the one eyebrow up" look, a sign that he was feeling simultaneously quizzical and annoyed. I argued in favor of buying so much candy since at least one of these bags would "definitely" be donated to the Redemption Center.

My ex said, "Fine," and I deposited the candy bags in our cart.

He lost me twice during that first supermarket excursion. I lagged, turning right or left depending on where my overstimulated brain would direct me to go. I kept thinking, how do people know what to buy? My ex bumped into me in one of the aisles; he had filled our cart with frozen French fries, frozen veggies and chicken nuggets, and several boxes of frozen pizza. My dream of living far away from any heat source, including the stove, was becoming a reality.

We added sodas to our cart and confidently approached the cashier. We flashed our smiles and greeted her with the enthusiasm we hoped would communicate our desire to belong to this great country, where we would extend our friendship to every American who crossed our paths.

The cashier spoke to us as she rang our purchases. We nodded yes to her questions paying close attention to her facial expressions, intermittently shaking our heads "no" if she looked alarmed at our silent acquiescence. We had agreed to contribute to a charity or two, and with tears in our eyes, we saw our names written on little flags that were now hanging from a string above the cashier's stand.

We felt ready for the Redemption Center! We exited the supermarket and stood at the entrance of the Redemption Center. We entered the large room where we could see some with a depository hole. The hole was too small to fit the candy and rice bags. We had tried, and now we looked around for machines with bigger holes. We were ready for Redemption; if only we could find the correct spot assigned for candy and dry goods donations. We did see some customers placing empty soda bottles in the machines. That didn't seem too charitable to us, but who are we to judge? We stood there pondering our options. I finally picked up two bags of candy and one of rice, leaving them on the empty counter, thinking that the redemption center attendant would know where to place our donation when he returned. We had only seen a few people come in with empty sodas. We considered that today may have been a slow donation day, but we were glad to contribute, especially on a slow day at the Redemption Center.

Feeling good about our generosity, we put our groceries in our superb Pontiac Grand Prix and drove away.

We came home excited after a very productive day. We put away the groceries and sat on the carpet facing our large glass sliding door that faced the wooded area.

We spoke about our day; my ex had placed the pizza in the oven. We sat looking at the sun setting behind the woods. As I waited for the pizza, I decided to call my mom in Brazil. She answered, thrilled to hear about our adventures and our newfound evidence of the fantastic American generosity. My dad shared the phone with my mom and listened intently to my supermarket/redemption story; he proclaimed, "America is amazing; you just have to look at their dollar bill where they write for everyone to see: 'In God we trust'!!"

They asked how everything else was going for us and if we had found a puppy to keep me company while my ex was in school. I had left my elderly poodle Mike in the home; he had grown up as my adored pet. Mike had shown a great dislike for my ex. On one occasion, Mike jumped up and ripped my ex's shirt pocket as my ex attempted to hug me. Mike loved my mom and dad; he was losing his vision, and staying back home was the right thing to do.

I missed my Mikey terribly; my ex had agreed that we would find a pup for me while he studied. He hoped that the new dog would be more accepting of him and his lack of familiarity with owning a pet. Our visa didn't allow me to work; I spent long hours alone.

My tone was somber when I told my parents what we found out about marriage in America while looking for a puppy in the local classifieds.

I told them about finding many puppies available, but sadly, they were from broken homes. The divorce rate in America must have been very high. We concluded that was the reason for so many "housebroken" puppies needing a home. My ex and I became determined to give one of these puppies a home with a solid marriage and the union intact. My ex vehemently agreed. Little did we know that five years later, our adopted puppy and my firstborn would also be living in a broken home.

We could smell the delicious pizza smell. I told my parents goodbye, promising to call them soon.

We ate the pizza, and it tasted slightly like cardboard. But we were famished and polished off most of it save for a few scraps of uneaten crust that I collected and threw outside our glass sliding door, hoping to give some birds a delicious treat. We had music on, and very soon, we had both dozed off in each other's arms on the carpet floor.

It was dark outside, and noises from outside the glass sliding door woke me up. I turned on the table lamp and looked in the direction of the noises. I became paralyzed, watching the creatures outside the glass door just a few feet away from us. I reached for my sleeping ex, keeping my eyes on the scene in front of me, ready to jump up and run if necessary. I tried to modulate my voice, trying not to scream, but what came out was a high-pitched screaming of my ex's name, followed by, "We have giant rats!!" My ex bolted upright; he looked at me and followed the direction.

I was pointing with my index finger. He let out a high-pitched scream of his own and yelled in Spanish, "No puede ser!" "This can't be!" We held each other while looking at several giant, gray-colored rats, who seemed unperturbed by our screams as they continued to eat the pizza scraps I had thrown in the garden for the birds.

My ex got up, walking towards the phone while I clung to his arm; while he reached for the phone, "We need the police," I said, "the rats may try to come in!" He dialed 911, attempting to sound calm. The dispatch asked in a monotone voice the reason for our call, my ex's name, and the address of the emergency, saying it in such a calm manner that caused my ex to think that perhaps he was not communicating the urgency of the situation. He shouted, "Help, big rat, our house, help." The police arrived at our door in minutes. We weren't sure why the fire department had also come to our rescue; my ex and I sighed with relief as we saw that one fire rescue person held an axe.

The commotion brought several onlookers to our apartment, including someone from management who was walking in for his evening shift. The fire and rescue officers stood next to two police officers as they looked at what was causing us terror. We stood behind them just in case we had to run for cover as soon as they opened the glass door and confronted the dangerous rats.

The firefighters started to leave the apartment; we could hear them laughing discreetly. The police officer told us that the creatures were harmless and called "opossums." He affirmed that they were not rats as I looked at the animals and their rat-like tails. They usually stay away from people; he continued that you may find them looking through garbage for food scraps late at night.

The officer approached the glass door, causing the opossums to scatter around. "I see that someone left them food," he said. I nodded yes to him and smiled innocently. We thanked the officers as they left, giving us a wave and telling us to "take care."

My ex closed the door and glared at me, shaking his head in disapproval of my interest in birds and animal encounters as long as they weren't reptiles or rodents. He mumbled in Spanish, "Vos con los animales, una loucura!" which meant "you and your craziness about animals!"

The residents had returned to their apartments, and the building manager left for his office, promising us to find who had left the food scraps outside our glass door.

I was left alone with the potential danger of dealing with my angry Argentinian. My ex's anger outbursts were from the textbook on "the Latino temper."

I hugged him and initiated a slow dance hoping to change his mood by appealing to his "Latino lover" side. He matched my body moves, and we danced. He locked our door, turning all the lights off. He joined me in our bed, his green eyes twinkling with desire, and as we embraced, he murmured in my ear, "Throw the food in the garbage next time." He had a way of keeping my emotions off balance, and I was never sure of his love or hate. I met his eyes, trying to draw an answer, hoping that the adage was true regarding "the eyes being the window of the soul." Like deep pools of light green, his eyes betrayed none of his secrets. Afterward, he brought the guidebook given to us at the BMV. He turned on his bedside light, and he went about the business of learning the American laws for drivers in Ohio.

# Chapter 4

*Driving Level Expert*

After recovering from our introduction to one of the many species of the urban fauna in Cincinnati, the unattractive but harmless possum, we spent the next few days before our scheduled return to the Bureau of Motor Vehicles studying our *OH Driver Mannual,* Spanish edition. My ex pored through the pages with the zeal usually reserved for sacred scriptures. I tried reading mine with the same enthusiasm; however, I was easily distracted by my thoughts which included my belief that I was a superb driver. This lack of humility originated from my experiences as a driver in the streets of São Paulo,in the 70s before cars with bulletproof glass. Brazilian drivers use a combination of mind reading, deep faith in the Lord and quick reflexes as they inch away through the red lights to avoid being mugged while simultaneously avoiding a collision with the drivers who speed through the green light.

São Paulo is a gigantic sprawling mish-mash of tall buildings, millions of miles of streets, avenues, and the famous "Minhocão."

The "Big Worm" was the suspended highway over São Paulo's busiest traffic areas. The drivers had the choice to climb on the giant worm from the access ramps, driving over the dense traffic, giving the driver an option to reach their destination closer to the ground or near the sky.

The "Minhocão" highway rested on tall cement structures that sadly gave way one day, killing most of the drivers that were going about their day driving on the suspended construction or under it.

That was a sorrowful day for São Paulo; the pride in the magnificent example of design and engineering turned into mourning for the victims and the survivors of this tragedy.

I learned how to drive with my older brother, whom I admired greatly. I thought of him to be an expert in everything. I was delighted by his attention and willingness to teach me how to drive while we were vacationing in "Ilha Bela" (a beautiful island) located an hour and a half from Sao Paulo.

I was thirteen years old, and my brother, who is eleven years my senior, had agreed to bring me along with his group of friends that had all grown up together in our town. Ilha Bela of the 70s was a Paradise with miles of beaches untouched by civilization. The dense forest served as the outdoor restrooms. We would walk into the woods carrying a toy shovel that we used to dig holes and then bury anything our bodies produced. The toy shovel was then rinsed with ocean water and laced back into the sand, where a paper flag marked the place for the shovel.

One day after we sat at camp, we watched one of my brother's best friends running from the forest, screaming as he plunged into the ocean after using a three-leaved plant as toilet paper, which he had forgotten to take with him as he hastily entered the woods. The salt in the ocean caused him to shout and run out of the sea. After running around a bit, he finally accepted the two large bottles of drinking water handed to him by my brother, the hero. His friend returned to the woods with the bottled water and rinsed himself. He required a trip to a pharmacy, and he spent the days at the beach inside his tent, reading books and lying on his stomach.

With his friend out of commission, my brother offered me some driving lessons on the deserted beach.

That afternoon, I was proudly sitting in the driver's seat of my brother's red VW bug. I felt so grown up.

The WV looked new; the red color had returned to its original state after a week at the repair shop, where they applied a fresh coat of paint. I was always looking for opportunities to show my brother how much I appreciated his time playing with me; the age difference could have made him wholly disinterested in me, just as my older sister seemed to be. My big sister spent hours fixing her hair and makeup and collecting shiny baubles that I was forbidden to touch.

My brother was away studying psychology at a university a few hours from our town. He would take a bus leaving his WV bug parked in our garage. I missed him dearly, and one day before his return home for the weekend, I decided to surprise my adored brother.

I found the floor wax in one of the closets; my reasoning for giving a wax job on my brother's car came from watching Geralda bring a sparkly shine to our parquet floors. I concluded that giving my brother's car a "good wax" would bring a beautiful glow to his red VW bug. No one was paying attention to my activities. Growing up in benevolent neglect allowed me to experiment with dangerous chemicals and explore anything I found intriguing.

I worked hard waxing every square inch of the VW bug under the hot Brazilian sun. I was sweating and nauseous, most likely due to the wax fumes. I looked at the red color on the VW bug, which strangely started to change into an opaque Maroon-pinkish color with circular grease spots made by the cotton rag I had used for the job. The car looked sort of good in my eyes, like a hippie vehicle, I thought to myself. My brother may like it or even love his polka-dot hippie-style VW bug.

I collected the empty wax tin and rags, throwing the whole mess in the building's trash. I walked the flight of stairs to our first-floor apartment, avoiding the elevator due to my petroleum smell. I showered for a long-time using lots of soap, shampoo, and scalding hot water to eliminate the odor.

I sat on my bed in my room and picked up one of my favorite books from the author Julio Gouveia. *Sitio do Pica Pau Amarelo.* The ranch of the yellow woodpecker that tells the story of a sweet but firm grandmother and her companion Tia Anastasia, a magnificent cook and doll maker. Her doll creations would come to life to the amazement of the lucky grandchild that lived at the ranch and her cousin who would come to stay on school vacation.

I lost myself in the stories of the magical adventures, where a fish prince lived in the pond where he would host a ball for all the creatures that lived in the pond and for the residents of the Yellow Woodpecker ranch including the sassy doll Emilia, The Sabugosa Viscount, a tall heat wearing corn husk creature who was somewhat of an intellectual with endless knowledge of all things inside his cob head. In the ranch creatures from the rich Brazilian folklore came out from the forest to play and scare the residents of the ranch.

I started to feel better after drinking several glasses of Kool-Aid and eating some snacks.

My thoughts were now reassuring me that my brother would appreciate my efforts and praise me for my work ethic and creativity.

That evening my parents and I sat by the open window, waiting for my brother to arrive. My parents sipped hot tea, affirming that the hot brew counteracted the heat and would actually "cool you down." I credit my parents' preposterous ideas for being the source of my wild hypotheses, creative thoughts, and concepts about the world around me.

My parents' ideas, which seemed to defy and contradict all logic, were their way to survive the concentration camps where logic did not guarantee survival. Their ability to elevate their thoughts and imagination to a place of hope allowed their spirit to continue fighting, animating their bodies into living another day.

My brother walked and placed his book bag on the floor. I hugged him excitedly and followed him to the kitchen, where he retrieved his car keys. He ate the food Geralda had left in the oven; my parents kept him company as he ate and told them about his studies. He finished his meal and went out to meet his friends, whom he would pick up on the way to the movies.

I seemed to have developed a case of traumatic amnesia about all the events that happened next.

I recall hearing my brother scream expletives from the parking lot, right below our first-floor apartment. My brother came back in, his face as red as the former color of his adored VW bug.

My parents walked down to the parking lot as I tip-toed back into my bedroom, realizing that my brother preferred his car to be in its original color.

My parents paid for the paint job and offered my brother to use their vehicle for his outing.

They banned me from entering the utility closets and every other room besides my bedroom without adult supervision.

The mandate lasted a week.

Life's busyness took away the adult's focus on me, and soon, the "wax the car" story was part of the thick volume of anthologies of my solitary childhood.

A few months after my "surprise," my brother and I were back on speaking terms, and there I was, beaming with excitement, ready for my first driving lesson.

My brother started the lesson by going through the complex order of events necessary to get a stick-shift car to move.

"That will require," he said calmly, "that you release the pressure on the brake pedal SLOWLY and simultaneously press your foot on the accelerator SLOWLY. You have to remember that the stick shift would need to go from the number 1 position to the number 2 to go faster, and you will go even faster by moving the stick shift to 3 and then 4, which is the car's fastest speed." And he continued, "You cannot forget to press the brake pedal between shift changes."

I looked at him, smiling, bobbing my head up and down in agreement with his instructions. I pushed down the accelerator and awkwardly let go of the brake pedal, failing to coordinate the complex balance of push and letting go slowly. The VW lurched forward with great force, and the engine died apparently in protest of this novice attempt at driving.

My brother sighed, and he repeated to me the whole sequence. The lesson lasted an entire afternoon. His friends kept waving to us from a distance, cheering for this important milestone in my life.

I drove a few times by the area where they stood, causing them to disburse, looking for a safe spot out of my way.

I continued to drive, which was still a bit bumpy for a while due to the lurches and sudden speed.

The engine would scream in protest, which reminded me that it was time to change gears.

By late afternoon, the sun started to set on the ocean; my brain seemed to have registered the driving sequence to a certain extent.

I parked the car near the tent, thinking about the sad fate of a few sand chickens in my path and feeling the start of a headache at the top of my head caused by driving fast on an embankment. The vehicle became airborne for a second before falling hard on the sand, causing us both to hit our heads on the car's ceiling.

My brother, at that point, declared the lesson to be over. He sat in the driver seat and drove us back to the camping site; I closed my eyes, enjoying the smooth ride and promising myself that I would one day achieve his expert driving skill level.

# Chapter 5

## *Laws, Not Suggestions*

In the following years, from the ages 13 to 18, the legal driving age in Brazil, I had accomplished my desired level of driving prowess, elegance, and comfort for myself and my passengers. I would take one of my parents' cars when they left together for an errand. I drove once around the block, returning the car to our parking spot in the building.

I became bolder, going for long drives every chance I got, taking advantage of the fact that laws in Brazil are up to your interpretation of them. I took them to be more like suggestions. Police traffic monitoring in Brazil was equally flexible.

In a traffic stop, the police and the driver would resolve the incident without the involvement of costly court proceedings or insurance.

A mutually agreed sum of money between the driver and the policeman would settle the matter in minutes.

Back in Cincinnati, my ex parked in front of the BMV building. We walked inside and stopped by the information desk, telling the attendant our names. Soon we were busy completing the written portion of the test. I looked at the multiple-choice questions with great relief. We both finished the written part, sharing a high five; we were jubilant; we had passed the written test.

I was looking forward to the driving test. I felt most confident and sat at the edge of the hard chairs at the BMV. My ex went first, following the apathetic-looking officer carrying a clipboard in one hand and what looked to be a stress ball in the other hand. I followed them outside, eager to familiarize myself with the process. The officer sat on the passenger seat of our Pontiac; my ex correctly deduced that he was to sit in the driver's seat, and after fastening his seat belt, he waved to me as he slowly pulled out of the parking spot.

They drove away, and he turned at the parking lot's exit; my ex had used the blinkers to announce the turn. I sat on the cement bench outside the building and fidgeted anxiously, waiting to see my ex-triumphant return. I started to worry when 45 minutes passed and there was no sign of the car. A couple of minutes later, I spotted my ex driving ever so slowly to the spot where he had parked before. The officer stepped out, scribbling something on the clipboard. He turned to face my ex and said, "You passed."

I was about to do a Brazilian celebratory dance, but I stopped, thinking I should wait until I had also passed the test.

My ex went inside the building to take a photo of the temporary license. I smiled at the officer as I waited for his instructions.

I couldn't wait for my turn driving, fully expecting an invitation to "join the force" after he saw my incredible driving abilities.

It bears repeating for those interested in visiting the Brazil that driving in most Brazilian cities will equip the motorist with the art of divination and superb driving skills of a Formula One driver. A would-be tourist should consider hiring a local driver and consult a doctor before the trip to make sure your heart is strong and your blood pressure is low.

. A local driver will know what to expect from the young men carrying spray bottles of soapy water that populate the stoplights. As you the car stops or slows down at the red light, they quicklyspray the windshield, and instead of a squeegee, you may find a handgun pointed at you, forcing you to hand them all your money and belongings and, at times, your car.

I sat in the driver's seat, ready to show off my extraordinary driving skills to the officer sitting next to me, holding the clipboard with both hands. I was about to pull out of the space when I heard a clicking sound. The officer pointed to my seat belt, still unfastened, and said, "Forgetting something?"

I pretended to adjust the seat and the mirror before reaching for my seatbelt and fastening it with a "click." I smiled at him, trying to establish a connection; he had an impenetrable look.

I looked back, watching for pedestrians walking in the parking lot; I pressed the gas pedal after shifting the gear in reverse and back to "drive" as I waited for the officer's directions.

He told me to turn right at the parking lot exit, and before he finished the sentence, I pressed the gas pedal and quickly gained speed. I held the wheel expertly with one hand as I used the other to arrange my hair; I turned right, and the car's tires let out a tiny screech. I went down the streets through stop signs, skillfully weaving in front of slow drivers, positioning my car leading traffic. I waited to hear more instructions from the officer, who clutched the clipboard with both hands; I noticed how pale his hands were, bulging white knuckles squeezing the clipboard.

I felt sympathy for the officer, thinking about his job and the anxiety he must feel driving with less experienced drivers than myself. The officer started to talk to me; he spoke fast, his voice getting progressively louder. I looked at him, trying to make out the words, causing him to point his finger forward, yelling, "Eyes on the road!" I began to feel that the driving test wasn't going as well as I thought it was.

I perceived the officer's rapid speech as a sign of excitement and admiration for the speed and accuracy of my well-timed stops. I had misread his animated facial expressions. His eyes were wide for what I took as amazement, and his mouth was agape, murmuring "shiiit" and "too fast." Thinking that he had said "go fast," I nodded, saying "fast, fast" while giving him the thumbs-up sign.

I returned to the BMV much faster than my ex. The whole circuit lasted 15 minutes or so. I was still hoping for a positive result. I even considered the possibility that I may have achieved some record in finishing a driver's test with the speed and accuracy of a professional driver. The officer opened his door and tried to walk out, forgetting to unbuckle himself.

He appeared agitated as he unfastened the seat belt and jumped out of his seat with remarkable athleticism. I exited the car and stood in front of the officer, smiling. He stared at me and said, "What was that?" He moved his hair from his forehead, smoothing back in place.

I asked the officer, "I pass"? He let out a scoff and then a laugh. I noticed sweat dripping down his forehead and shirt collar, which appeared to have collected a large amount of moisture.

He walked into the building. I followed him, unsure of what to do. He placed the clipboard on the counter and walked to a water cooler that stood in the corner. He returned, still holding the plastic cup from where he took small sips. I waited to hear that I had passed the test. My ex joined me at the counter, asking me in English, "Pass, pass test?" I nodded enthusiastically, unsure but hopeful. We looked at the stunned officer, who most likely had never experienced anything like he had encountered that day.

The officer had regained his composure; he handed me the paper from the clipboard where I could see the x in the space next to the word "Fail." I was still under the magical powers of denial, and I asked, "Good,"? The officer appeared exasperated by the language barrier; he repeated, "No good, no pass." My heart sank as he declared that my driving was "appalling ", he tried to communicate with me in my version of the English language, " No Pass!."

The realization that I had failed the driving test was slowly sinking in. Dread and disbelief had us standing at the counter unmoving. My ex and I spoke to each other and started collaborating in constructing a sentence made from the English words each knew. We needed to ask what happens after failing the driver's test; would my ex have to drive me around for as long as we lived? We both shuddered at the thought.

The officer returned with another official who introduced himself as officer Perez in perfect-sounding Spanish!

People close to where we stood were watching us, interested in the unfolding story, like a "telenovela" at the BMV. Officer Perez read the notes left by the other officer written on the paper he had given me with the "fail" result.

He asked me, "Did you see the stop sign?"

"Si, I saw it," I answered.

He continued, "But you didn't stop!"

I said, "No, I didn't have to because there were no other cars around!"

Officer Perez exchanged a glance with the driving officer; who said, "See what I mean"?

Officer Perez continued. "You ignored the speed limit signs of the allowed speeds in certain zones."

""I did not ignore the signs, I said with the outrage of the innocent, "I thought those were suggestions! the sign suggests you go 30 miles, which seems to imply that ifthere are no cars around, you can go faster, right?."I asked triumphantly as I felt I made a lot of sense.

Officer Perez and the other officer answered in unison, "wrong"! I heard the words being exchanged between them "Unbelievable, and this must be some sort of a prank."

Officer Perez retrieved another copy of the *OH Driver's Manual* and placed it on the counter. "I will set up another driver's test exam in a week for you to take. You study the manual again; these are laws, not suggestions." I picked up the manual, and my ex and I thanked officer Perez for his help.

I was relieved to get a second chance at driving legally in America. I followed my ex to our car, expecting a "Que te passa?" showdown with my ex, complete with hand gestures and a long sermon. My ex sat in the car; I sat by him, my eyes wheeling with tears. He surprised me with a hug and said, "You will pass the test next time."

This unexpected show of love and understanding from my usually reserved ex brought on a full ugly cry with hiccups and a runny nose as he held me in his arms. I calmed down, and he patted me on the head, a gesture that always annoyed me. That day I did not protest. I relaxed in my seat and looked at the trees and the stop signs and speed limit signs, noticing them for the first time since coming to America.

I felt like I just had a breakthrough; laws in America, unlike in Brazil, are expected to be followed and are not up for your interpretation! I had just survived my first cultural shock. I congratulated my ex for getting the driver's license. I leaned back on the seat, thinking to myself, "What a day!" I felt something on my back; I reached behind, finding the well-used stress ball the officer had in his hand at the start of my driving. I squeezed it and told myself that this ball would be a great reminder of today's failure. I will return it to its rightful owner in a week.

# Chapter 6

---

## *Jerry Springer And The Chili Show*

A week went by when my days were consumed in learning and memorizing every rule of the road contained in the *Ohio Driver's Manual*. My ex nodded in approval as I held the little book in my hands with the same passion he had while studying for the test two weeks ago. He will take me driving in the mall parking lot, confessing for the first time that my driving "made him nervous."

I drove around the parking lot, carefully observing the speed limit and expertly avoiding the shoppers pouring in and out of the mall.

I would park the car in the parking spot only to pull out again after a second. I would drive around, looking for a place to practice backing the vehicle in reverse.

After driving for an hour or so, repeating the maneuvers in different areas of the parking area, we stopped to rest a bit and decide what to do next. A man wearing a blue uniform approached us.

He introduced himself as the "mall security" and asked if we required assistance in helping us find the entrance to the mall or the exit from the parking lot. I was, once more, amazed at how caring Americans are!

I explained to the security person the purpose of my activities in the parking lot, reassuring the mall security that we were not drunk, lost, or indecisive. He touched his hat in a mini salute and returned to his post.

I looked at my watch; the time was 1:15 PM, and my stomach was growling. My ex walked around the car and opened the door for me to step out; he would be driving us somewhere to eat. I sat on the passenger side, yet the vehicle did not move.

I looked at my ex, wondering, what now? The driving lesson was over, and I wanted food! I thought to myself, what did I miss? "Ah," I said, "I forgot to lock the door!" I checked the door and locked it.

We were still not moving. I smiled, looking at my ex adoringly, who I thought felt a sudden wave of passion as he moved his left arm across my chest. I wasn't about to miss responding to what I thought was a romantic moment. I turned my body towards him and placed my arms around his shoulders. I offered him my lips, ready for a kiss. Instead, my ex gave me a coughing sound as he stared at me. He pushed me back and said, "You forgot the seat belt again." I laughed awkwardly in embarrassment at my absent mind and for reading too much into his arm gesture.

Brazilians are prone to sudden moments of passion while performing mundane tasks. Argentinians, not so much, at least not my Argentinian.

We pulled out from our spot and drove around the college area, looking for a restaurant. We passed a sign that read "Skyline Chili, home of the authentic Cincinnati Chili."

The picture in the window showed a dish piled high with cheese, which fit one of my criteria for yummy food.

My ex read the sign advertising the dish, which consisted of "mounds of steaming spaghetti and original-secret recipe." We looked at each other, agreeing to go taste the secret recipe.

We entered the brightly lit restaurant. My ex ordered two

Skyline Chili with "everything" at the counter and sat next to me in our booth.

I was watching a group of people having an animated discussion. One of them looked familiar to me; I tried to remember where I heard his distinctive voice and saw his face.

My ex elbowed me on my side and said, "Que te passa, why are you staring"?

"Oh," I told my jealous Latino ex, "I think I recognize the man in the suit."

The individual in question wore a well-tailored dark suit. His sandy hair was styled into a slight bouffant.

The man would greet the people who entered the establishment, who had also recognized him, and he was soon surrounded by what appeared to be fans. Some shook his hand before finding their seats, while others patted his back, exclaiming, "Hey, Jerry"! excitedly.

Suddenly it came to me; I could hear his nightly farewell to his listeners on the nightly news: "Take care of yourselves and each other, good night!" I have always felt so comforted by his words.

I elbowed my ex back and said, "The guy from the news!! Jerry Springer!!" He was a celebrity. Years later, we moved to Holyoke, Massachusetts; I remember watching a few episodes of *The Jerry Springer Show*.

I would shake my head in utter disbelief that Jerry had left serious journalism for a tv show where the guests ran around while being chased by another guest or two. Other times, the guest would run around in circles before collapsing on the ground, pounding their fists in protest over alleged misdeeds or the unexpected revelation regarding being thrust into paternity after a casual encounter.

The words "You are the father" would cause the audience to jeer at the male guests, who would lower their heads in shame and, at times, drop to their knees as the accusing party beat them over their heads while yelling, "I told you!!" until security would intervene while Jerry retreated away from the spectacle. There were other instances when the guests would hear, "You are not the father." The words would cause another uproar from the audience.

The relieved guest would run around like Rocky Balboa, jumping and showing intricate dancing steps while exchanging "high fives" with some male audience members.

Gone were the days of Jerry's kind and thoughtful message, telling his news audience to "Take care of yourselves and each other, good night." *The Jerry Springer Show* would end with camera shots of the guests still fighting.

The spectators reluctantly would get up from their seats, walking single file towards the exit, their heads turned towards the set, attempting to get the last glimpse of the show's guests. Jerry would leave the stage first, escorted by two burly security men. Jerry's face showed relief and a worn-out sadness.

I wondered if Jerry missed being a news reporter, sitting at his desk sharing the news with the female news reporter, laughing and exchanging clever banter, and turning solemn when the information was terrible.

I wondered if he missed being the mayor of Cincinnati.

Several years later, I read some distressing news about his conduct. I was sad for my first American celebrity. I wondered if being surrounded by mendaciousness and scandal had somehow impacted his moral compass. There were other similar shows.

I occasionally watched *Sally Jesse Raphael*, a belittling blond woman wearing red-rimmed glasses. She would openly mock some of her guests while looking at the audience for approval. They would cheer and laugh at the guests who sat uncomfortably facing the audience.

I would always anticipate Sally's compassionate act for her guests, who were usually victims of some horrendous act. Suddenly a sad melody would start playing in the background, and on cue, Sally's eyes would well up in tears, and she would offer a half-hearted hug or pat on her guest's back, who would return a hopeful gaze at Sally and her audience. My all-time favorite was Phil Donahue; I learned a lot of English by watching his show. He seemed a bit more genuine than Sally.

Back in Cincinnati, we were about to taste the chili brought to us by the server.

We both examined the steaming dish in front of us; Jerry Springer had already left, waving back to the customers, us included, chiming into the shouts of "Take care, Jerry!" as he exited the building.

There was nothing else to do but concentrate on the Skyline Chili.

Food portions in America were gigantic when compared to those in Brazil. I pondered about what would be the "right approach" to consume the food structure in front of me.

I could mix it all, the cheese evenly distributed instead of just sitting at the top. How about the brown meat? Could this be a Bolognese sauce? After all, 70 percent of the dish was spaghetti. I looked around discretely after pretending to have dropped my paper napkin. From that angle, I could see the other customers twirling their forks into the dish and expertly balancing spaghetti, meat, and cheese into their mouths. I was picking up my napkin from the ground when I looked at my ex's eyes as he had dunked his head under the table, looking to see if I needed his assistance.

I sat back in my seat, ignoring him and looking at the untouched food in front of me. The smell of this dish confused me; it made me think of faraway lands in the Orient mixed with Western Europe and Latin America. Regarding food, I have always needed sensory input to help the communication between my brain and my belly. For instance, if I smelled pizza, my brain would tell my stomach, "Pizza experience located, good experience, go ahead and enjoy it."

I had a vast catalog of smells, sights, and tastes associated with my brain's reliable alert system that would encourage me to "go ahead, eat this food" and "danger, danger, stay away, uniden-tified and scary ingredients!"

My ex's brain circuit regarding food was less sensitive than mine. My ex had already devoured half of the chili mound; he gave me a thumbs up and then pointed to my plate, saying the customary "Que te passa?"

I picked up the fork and aimed it at the middle of the chili mountain; I twirled the spaghetti cheese and meat and brought it to my mouth; the spiciness that my brain had detected earlier in the chili smell was now invading my taste buds, causing my throat to close up. I placed the fork on my plate and discretely deposited the contents of my mouth on the napkin.

That was my first and last bite of chili ever. The Skyline secret sauce was still burning my mouth. I proceeded to drink my water, refilling it several times from the water pitcher they had brought to the table. My ex looked at me as I coughed and sneezed from the spices in the food. He passed me the bread basket and told me to have a bite. "The food is a bit spicy," he conceded.

My ex had finished his chili, and I noticed a look of regret as he reached for some bread, washing it down with a few glasses of water. Each table had a large water pitcher available to the customers so they could save themselves from spontaneous human combustion.

We left the Skyline restaurant and slowly walked towards the car. My ex walked a bit hunched over, feeling the first signs of heartburn and other gastric phenomena. I was still gnawing at the pieces of bread, finally recovering some feeling in my tongue.

We decided to skip the mall and my driving lessons.

My ex parked the car in our apartment complex; he jumped out and yelled, "I have to go," and ran up the stairs, unable or unwilling to wait for the elevator.

I decided against joining him in the apartment, knowing my ex would appreciate my absence as he dealt with the aftermath of the chili in private.

I walked a few laps in front of our garden floor apartment, keeping an eye on the sliding doors.

After 20 minutes or so, I saw my ex, sweaty, waving to me from the open window of our bedroom.

The Tums bottle was half empty on the kitchen counter. My ex lay on the sofa, still diaphoretic and pale. I turned on the TV and sat by his side. His stomach gurgled from time to time. My ex fell asleep on the sofa, his mouth open, probably enjoying the cooling effects of the night air after surviving eating lava.

# Chapter 7

## *Sheets*

My ex had entirely recovered by the next day. He was not interested in talking about the experience at Skyline Chili, and I let it go, recognizing the look of someone who has gone through a traumatic event. We sat together, sipping coffee and going through the newspaper; my ex would try to remain current with the news around the world with the help of the trusty English/Spanish dictionary by his side and a cool gadget, The Franklin Pocket Translator Spanish/English. We spent hours marveling at the American ingenuity in creating small machines that knew languages. That afternoon, we would take the little gadget on our first shopping trip to JCPenney, the famous American store.

We walked in through the shoe department; we were soon overwhelmed by the enormous variety of inventory, from shoes to garden equipment. We stumbled onto the bedroom apparel session, which had been the reason for going to the department store. My ex wrote the word "Sabanas" on the little gadget that instantly told us that we were looking for bed sheets."

We approached the customer service counter, and a pleasant-looking middle-aged lady quipped with great sincerity, "Welcome to JC Penny!"

We both responded in the same effusive tone, "Thank you, thank you."

My ex held up the gadget and read the word "bed sheets." We conferred on the correct pronunciation of words with a double "E"; and listened to the device's accent. The sound clarity on portable devices at that time was somewhat poor.

We went with our best possible guess opting to add a bit of a British accent for good measure. My ex cleared his throat and told the lady at the counter: "want baad shaats," elongating his vowels, which we thought sounded close to the device's pronunciation of the word "bed sheet." We added the verb as is used in Spanish.

We stood there smiling and repeating our request while adding helpful visuals to clarify our request. My ex and I put our hands by our faces as we pretended to lay on a pillow, sleeping angelically. She looked at us and said, "I beg your pardon?" We looked at each other, confused by her response. Why was she begging our pardon?! I reassured her that she was pardoned; however, we still needed new sets of bedding and blankets. We repeated our pantomime, assuming a sleeping pose by putting our hands as if we were praying and sleeping simultaneously. This time I tried reversing the order of the words and said: "Sheet bed, please." And added, "Por favor."

Seeing that the lady at the counter still had a stunned expression, my ex handed her the device so she could read and see that our request was very reasonable. In retrospect, that would have made things go a lot smoother. The lady's face brightened with a smile and then, to our surprise, changed into a loud laugh.

She was still laughing and motioned us to follow her to the store section marked "Bedding," where we found a large selection of "sheet beds" or "bed sheets."

The customer service lady said in between bouts of laughter, "You are looking for 'bed sheets.'" Her pronunciation was markedly different than ours. She left us, walking away with her laughter trailing after her.

She returned a few minutes later and gave us an impromptu English lesson. She handed us a notepad where she had written, "Sheets and bed are for sleeping." We nodded our heads and moved on to the words; she pointed using her pen to the other words she had written on the notepad. She lowered her voice to a whisper and said, "Shat and shit only in the bathroom." My ex typed the word "shit" in the portable translator device and showed it to me next.

We nodded in agreement, mortified. We finally realized that our pronunciation had given the impression that we suffered from bowel incontinence in the best-case scenario and the worst-case that shitting in bed was our preference.

We thanked the customer service lady for her kindness in going so far as to explain the gross misunderstanding of our initial request.

She walked back to her post, and we quickly made our selections, paying for them at a register and exiting the store without suffering further embarrassment.

We drove to the Bureau of Motor Vehicles for my second attempt at obtaining my driver's license.

I was happy to have the same officer with the white knuckles accompany me on round 2. I sat in the driver's seat and fastened my seat belt, smiling at the officer who was fastening his seat belt and holding the clipboard in one hand and the other in the "assist grip." That reminded me of his stress ball that I retrieved from the back seat and handed to the officer. He thanked me, placed the ball in his jacket pocket, and resumed holding on to the assist grip.

He took a deep breath and said, "Let's start."

I backed out slowly, and this time, I drove at the exact "suggested" driving speed, stopping at a stop sign and waiting until a car appeared to proceed, showing my understanding of the stop sign dynamics. The officer cleared his throat after we sat in the empty intersection for a few minutes, telling me, "You can go now."

I observed the speed limit, and after 45 minutes, I drove back to the BMV; the officer had removed his sweaty hand from the "assist grip" handle and wrote on the clipboard before telling me, "You passed the test." I was so happy! I walked back to the BMV office, proudly giving my ex the thumbs-up sign of victory. He had chosen to wait in the office for my return. I had my temporary driver's license.

I was ready for the American roads. Or so I thought.

I still insisted on driving us home. I didn't care; I had accomplished my goal.

I rested my head against the seat, dreaming of driving my American-made Pontiac Grand Prix with automatic transmission, enjoying the allowed speed on the highways. I tried to recall the highway speed I had read in the manual. Was it 80 or 90 KM an hour? No, not KM. Miles. I made a mental note to check the driver's manual at some point.

I closed my eyes while listening to our radio /cassette system.

"Gracias a la Vida, Que me ha dado tanto," Mercedes Sosa sang in her rich and deep voice, the words to the melody, "Thank you, life, for giving me so much." I started to sing with Mercedes, managing to utter two words of the lyrics before hearing my ex clearing his throat, a signal used to convey his annoyance at my singing performance.

I stopped and hugged my paper driver's license. I would soon be driving alone in the car, and then I will sing. Oh yes, I will sing.

# Chapter 8

## *The Place I Don't Belong*

Back in our little apartment in Cincinnati, my ex and I spent the weekend debating on the American dream of home ownership.

We had a savings account where the money gifted by our parents and other generous relatives stayed untouched.

My ex-short-living stint as a "Marchand" or "Art dealer" had proved that acquiring art that was beautiful and valuable in our eyes would not translate into profit and a successful break into the art business. My ex's dream was to host fancy "soirees" filled with art connoisseurs and lay people willing to discuss literature, philosophy, and art. The guests would eat delightful canapes and other finger foods and drink Chilean wine and Veuve Clicquot Champagne.

Then dazzled by the beautiful art pieces and the wine, the lucky guests would get a chance to pay top dollar for our exclusive curated collection of completely unknown Brazilian artists.

The business plan lacked knowledge and connections in the art world, and after a while, funds, as the art collection grew, but sales never came to fruition.

The whole enterprise managed to produce one sale, a miniature 18th-century European oil painting given to us by my aunt, my mom's sister. My ex's commission from the sale was as small as the painting, which marked the end of his short-lived art dealer career.

My ex certainly "looked the part" as he dressed in carefully assembled outfits, his beard expertly trimmed. He would sometimes blow dry his hair into an impressive crown of light brown hair which contrasted nicely with his reddish-blond beard and watery green eyes.

As the Fall started in Ohio, he would wear beige wool cardigans and an ascot necktie. He was trim and very tall; his elegant figure would turn the heads of women and men alike as we shopped at Kroger.

He stood out in a sea of casually dressed individuals, myself included. I had always been laid back in my style of dressing and styling my long hair. My ex would encourage me to be more mindful when putting together my outfits. He once told me that a Farrah Fawcett haircut would make me look stunning. I would make an effort, and my ex would take me shopping, making the clothing selections on my behalf. I would try on the clothing at home and look in the mirror, looking for a glimpse of myself hiding behind the clothes of his selection.

My ex and I spent the weekends antiquing, which meant buying old things due to our level of knowledge in identifying priceless antiques. One weekend we drove by a sign that announced "flea market." My ex typed the words in the trusty portable translator as a precaution in case the poster was a warning for the shoppers about the possible presence of fleas in the merchandise.

We were relieved by learning through the translator device that this was not the case. We confidently entered the flea market and spent hours perusing the stands, hoping to find antiques worth millions.

My ex had a book about signature marks, usually found at the bottom of a vase or figurine, and at times, there will be no signature at all. Only an art connoisseur could recognize the valuable art of the humble artist that decided against spoiling his creation by including branding of his name.

We had tried our hand at the money-making schemes and yielded no returns; we decided we needed to make a solid investment in our future. After a few weeks of landing in Ohio, homeownership and the American dream became our dream.

We felt that purchasing a home was wise as we expected to stay in Ohio for at least two years as my ex worked on his Master's degree. We learned that the Cincinnati area homes were out of our budget, and we couldn't work on student Visas. We had a modest income from our rented apartment in São Paulo, which had been our parents' wedding gift. We lived there briefly before deciding to embark on our American experience.

We looked in Cincinnati's surrounding areas, with the circle of affordability becoming wider and wider.

The thought of my ex having to commute to school daily while I was left behind living alone somewhere in the Ohio countryside was exciting to us. We were clueless, and we had the energy and enthusiasm of the young.

We drove to our first showing of a property 45 minutes from the University. We followed the car of our new second best friend made in America, the real estate agent.

Like our first friend, the car salesman, the real estate agent had received us with the warmth of a long-lost relative recently found.

The real estate agent was a tall red-headed man wearing a suit that tightly hugged his portly frame.

We had arrived at the entrance to the property, the leaves in the trees that tickly lined both sides of the gravel road had turned yellow and several hues of red. We looked at the beauty of the Fall leaves, stunned delight, smitten by the lushness and vibrant colors. We had not thought about seeing the same entrance, lined with trees devoid of all foliage, standing naked and tall, looking ominous and bleak in the Winter that would follow.

The house was a brown-trimmed brick "ranch." We had hoped to see some evidence of pastures, with saddled horses waiting tied to the posts for the cowboy, as we had seen in movies depicting ranches.

This first contender in our quest for homeownership was a 33-acre property. There were no stables or horses. The house was the only building in the vast area, which was much less attractive in person than in the real estate catalog.

Seeing the house up close caused me to feel a shiver down my spine. My gut instinct perked up, signaling me with the unmistakable feeling that usually predicted "trouble" with incredible accuracy. Growing up in Brazil, developing a keen instinct for trouble or danger was a necessary adaptive skill that assured your survival in the streets of São Paulo. The survival of both body and spirit in my childhood home had also developed early.

My mother, who had superiors instincts that kept her alive at The Majdanek concentration camp at the age of thirteen was a phenomenal risk assessor and a human lie detector who, could read "a guilty" expression a mile away She would demand to know the the crime she suspected had been comitted "this instant," she would chase the alleged culprit as she menacingly held her slipper. The guilty party, usually me, would run around the large dining room table, refusing to heed her order to "Stop so I can hit you." My mom would eventually throw the slipper at me, carefully not to hit my head, abandoning the chase and going to her bedroom to rest. Many years later, my mother would amaze me with her detective skills that would catch my ex with his hand inside a cookie jar holding on to several cookies at the same time, so to speak… My siblings, on rare occasions, would incur her wrath; they would never run from her, despite their awarenessof my mother's intent to use her slipper as a "weapon," their acceptance of their fate was always a mystery to me. My siblings, eleven and twelve years older than me, would stand and wait for the promised action which was more yelling and slipper waving than a actual beating I would watch my compliant siblings in amazement wanting to tell them, "She is telling you she is going to hit you, run!"

My mom was approaching her forties, and I guess she would tire out quickly from chasing me. She would notify me from her bedroom that I had "given her a headache," and she would now wait for my dad to return home, saying he would "deal with me."

I had no genuine concern regarding my dad "dealing with me" as he was the calmest and sweetest man alive.

I had to concentrate on appeasing my mom's rattled nerves. The sequence of events was always the same.

I would sit outside her bedroom door for at least ten minutes, and after I felt that she had regained her composure, I would gently knock at the door, offering my apologies and a cup of tea to treat her "headache."

This ritual continued for many years until my wedding and departure to America.

As I faced the ranch's front door, I shook my head and forced myself to concentrate back on the present.

The front door was a pumpkin orange color to match the bricks and the dark brown trim. The real estate agent was addressing us in a very cheerful way, enthusiastically pointing to the "selling points" of this "once-in-a-lifetime opportunity." My ex listened intently, shifting his gaze to look at the acreage on a map that the real estate broker pulled from his pocket.

The real estate agent had sensed my lack of enthusiasm and detected a look of apprehension and doubt on my face.

He was now talking about how "lucky" we were to have reached out to him, who has brought us to see this "once-in-a-lifetime opportunity" to own "prime land" and blah, blah, blah, he had my ex transfixed, and I was nauseous.

I tried to quiet the rising anxiety in my chest; I tugged at my ex's sleeve. I had been sufficiently alarmed to forget how my ex detested that I touched in that manner.

I ignored his annoyed look and asked him to walk with me for a minute. I led him away from the realtor. I tried to find the words to convey my fears in a detached manner, preferred by my ex.

When I disclosed to him my gut feeling, his eyes rolled to the back of his head, and he dismissed my anxiety by asking if I was hungry or if it was "that time of the month." I should have known better. My ex started to walk back to continue his chat with our second-best friend in America, who looked at me triumphantly as my ex asked him, "Can we see inside?" The realtor agreed and walked with my ex to the front door for the second time. I followed my ex slowly, feeling defeated and slightly ashamed at my reluctance to ignore a "feeling" without having a fact attached.

I decided to look at this once-in-a-lifetime opportunity with clarity and resolve. After all, this was the first and only house we had visited so far, and no one buys the first house they see without seeing other homes for comparison.

I was so happy with my reasoning. There will be no more requests for validation or further discussions regarding "gut feelings."

I told myself I would base my concerns and opinions only on facts.

I looked at my ex confidently as I prepared myself to join him in the world of logic and rationale. I tucked away my internal dialogue and my instinct in a safe place, away from judgment and ridicule.

I could foresee my ex's and my relationship growing as we stood together in the "fact-based reality." I saw the orange door slowly opening after the broker's insistent knocking for a long time.

I took a deep breath and told my intuition, "I will listen to you later."

# Chapter 9

## *The Ranch*

The real estate agent knocked at the door for quite a long time. We could hear the muffled sounds of people talking to each other, followed by noises of heavy objects being shifted in a hurry, landing with loud thumps. The agent smiled nervously and knocked again.

"Hi, we are here for our appointment." I tried again to meet my ex's gaze, hoping to communicate the slight panic in my chest. Still, my ex's attention was now on the large open garage door, showing the smooth concrete floor, a few shelves, and a washer and dryer unit pushed against the wall. Three red steps led to the entrance to the kitchen. My mind was now swirling with memories of the American horror movies dubbed in Portuguese that I had watched in the safety of my childhood home, where my parents were one scream away from coming to rescue me.

My mom and dad had formidable courage as they fought real monsters while attempting to survive in the concentration camps. Nothing much rattled their nerves other than their memories of the camps triggered by seemingly innocuous sounds like someone wearing wooden clogs. I remember begging my mom for a pair of Dr. Scholl's clogs that all my friends were wearing, but she refused.

I was mad, telling her with the utter self-centeredness of a teenager that she was "ruining my life."

One day, exhausted by another bout of "please buy me the clogs," my mom removed both of her shoes she placed them next to me on the sofa where I sat. She showed me three of her toes in each foot that had become frozen and was now permanently numb and painful due to wearing wooden open-toed clogs during the brutal European Winters. The practical and thrifty German camp commanders would save the clogs from the dead, passing them on to those still alive and able to walk. Death was the expectation in the camps; remaining alive was considered a fluke, a momentary lapse in attention from death.

During the Winter, on especially frigid nights, the laughing guards would wake up the walking skeletons for surprise "exercises," which consisted of having the prisoners carry heavy boulders from one side of an open area and back to where the boulders stood in the first place.

In the morning, my mother and the other prisoners would walk in the snow and ice from the barracks to the ammunition factory, where my mom and the other prisoners would fill bullets with lead and other chemicals by hand. Her fingerprints were almost nonexistent when she and my aunt's sister were liberated.

Years later, my parents moved to the US after my siblings and I moved there. My mother's fingerprints would come into question after a few months; she provided the fingerprints on her Visa application. She called me to tell me about the "very nice FBI agents" that knocked at the door of her Miami apartment.

My diminutive mother invited the tall agents inside and asked them to sit while she made tea and served the cookies. My mother ignored their refusal of food and beverages and returned to sit on the sofa after placing a large plate of almond cookies and her best tea set on the coffee table in front of the agents.

One of the agents gave my mother documentation that explained their visit. My mother's lack of visible fingerprints on several of her digits was of concern for the American immigration Taskforce, which would investigate cases of fugitives that may have attempted to erase their digitals.

My mother retrieved her documents showing her record of being a slave worker in an ammunition factory and a prisoner in Majdanek.

My mother was always ready for a joke to lighten up the sad reality of her past, quipped, "It's ok, I can kill somebody and get away with it! Ha, ha," she laughed, stopping as soon as she noticed no one had joined her. The agents again refused the tea and cookies and left after apologizing for the inconvenience.

My mother, still unsure what to say, told them in her broken English and Brazilian hospitality to "come back soon!" While speaking to me on the phone after they had left, she was outraged about their refusal to partake in the refreshments until I reminded her that no one would touch any food or drink after hearing the hostess boast about getting away with murder.

My mom's sister had been a nurse before the war. She was assigned to care for the dead and dying in the camp infirmary for the slave laborers of the ammunition factory. My aunt kept my mom alive by feeding her scraps from the meager rations given to the ill in the infirmary. My mom had consumed food left by those dying of Typhus. She did not become infected with the deadly disease.

She had always made me feel safe by protecting me from anything real. My father's tenderness and unmovable faith in the higher power tackled the spiritual and the imaginary.

My father's faith kept his fellow prisoners in Buchenwald confused by his refusal to lose his humanity and descend into despair. My father was joyful in the most hopeless of places. He would sit on the ground, spreading the scraps of food he could find that day, inviting his stupefied companions in misery to sit and partake in the food he found.

He would take only a tiny portion to himself, and after blessing the food, he would eat it, still motioning those around him to sit and eat. "Why do you do this, you fool?" some would tell him. "How do you know you will ever find food again"? My father would smile, his blue eyes narrowed by his laughter as he would touch his chest and say,"I know the Lord Almighty will keep me safe until we are free, I know," he would repeat. He would stand after he had consumed his portion, saying, "The almighty God will get me out of this place; stick by me, and we will walk to freedom together."

These memories came to me as we waited for the ranch's front door to open. A tall, dark-haired man finally opened the front door; he had long brown hair and a beard. He and his brothers, had the same long hair and beard, Beatles style, apart from one who appeared to have stopped his barber in the middle of his haircut before he could chop the long hair in the back. I learned later that it was cut like that on purpose in a style popular at that time described as "serious in the front and party in the back."

They were all wearing flannel shirts and jeans; they all stood, staring at us in brooding silence.

The shorthair/long hair brother was in charge of answering the questions posed by the realtor, who would, in turn would convey the answers to my ex and me in a lively manner, pointing out the "selling points" of this property. The real estate broker spent a considerable amount of time pointing to the large brick fireplace where the head of one of my favorite characters from the Disney movie "Bambi" stared blankly from a wooden frame its mouth slightly open as if about to beg for his life or warn us to run for ours.

We continued the tour to the open kitchen where mustard yellow counters held the remnants of a meal, and one single fork stood up, piercing a slab of meat. I looked for signs of other plates and cutlery, distracted by the mental image of the four brothers taking turns using the single fork, all eating from that serving platter of brown meat.

My ex and the realtor walked down a hall towards the bedrooms.

The carpet looked like a replica of the hallway carpet in the movie The Shining. The brown doors to the three back bedrooms and one bathroom were closed. As the agent approached the first door to the only "suite," he opened the door slowly, carefully, and deliberately as if he expected "something" to jump out at him with a screech.

The suite had olive-green shaggy carpet that appeared to have missed a good vacuum cleaning since installed several decades ago. The brown queen-sized bed faced two windows showing the backyard with overgrown bushes. I looked out the window at the flat open space, which appeared to have been used to plant corn at one time.

The terrain had trees flanking each side of the open area and more trees to the back. The view from the window did not help the weight resting in the pit of my stomach. The trees appeared to creep into the open area menacingly.

I walked into the bathroom suite and faced the olive-green toilet, strangely small and low in height. The sink was also green. The drab showerhead stood above the olive-green bath-tub. The shower curtains with yellow ducks completed the bath-room decor. I am sure my facial expressions betrayed my true feelings of complete disgust. The concept of fixing it and flip-ping, doing it all yourself, was still years away.

The realtor sensed my desire to run out of the house scream-ing. He turned around and walked us out of the "suite" to see the rest of the place. Two small bedrooms and a bathroom completed the 1600-square-foot ranch.

We moved towards the kitchen and passed by the silent broth-ers, whose eyes followed us. I had lagged and attempted to smile at the brothers as I passed them, their matching flat expressions did not betray a hint of the most basic of human non-verbal communication, a smile. I felt a shudder, and I hurried up to the kitchen, where the real estate agent held open the door leading to the garage. He exalted the features of the oversized garage and the washer and dryer, which he continued, would be all "included" with the green refrigerator and green stove with the purchase of this property. My ex, at this point, had walked out of the garage, calling me to follow him outside which I did in a hurry ready to tell him how I really felt about the creepy house with the creepy brothers and the poor deer hanging from the fireplace. We stood in the gravel area, my ex lit a cigarette and said, "Soo? What do you think"?

Before I could answer; he took the rolled-up real estate magazine from his back-pants pocket.

My ex pointed to the ad he had circled with a pen. The ad read, "ranch with 33 acres, your paradise and hunting land."

"This is a bargain," he affirmed, excitedly puffing away on his cigarette. "We will own land," he exclaimed, sounding like Scarlett O'Hara in the movie *Gone with the Wind*.

I swallowed hard, trying to keep my emotions in check, knowing that if I mentioned anything regarding "gut feelings," my ex would shut me down with "you and your superstitions."

He waited, staring at me, looking to hear my enthusiastic remarks regarding the property.

I looked at the open space leading to the trees; I thought about my ex, growing up in a small apartment with his sister and parents on a busy street in Buenos Aires. I understood his dreams of success in America, where home ownership is the first step to prosperity. We were still years away from understanding that the bank granting us a mortgage meant they owned the property, not us.

The real estate agent approached us and excused himself for having to leave for another appointment.

My ex looked at me, pleading for my support in realizing his dream. My ex smiled and took me by the hand giving it a reassuring squeeze.

I sighed and whispered to him, "Ok, let's do it." He dropped the cigarette on the ground, stepping on it carefully to extinguish any sparks that would pose a fire threat to our own "paradise and hunting land."

My ex shook the hand of the realtor and said, "We want to buy it." The realtor shook my ex's hand excitedly; he seemed extremely surprised by our quick decision after seeing just one property which betrayed our lack of judgement and extremely poor insight. He turned around to see the brothers standing together and gave them a thumbs-up signal.

My ex and I walked hand in hand to our car. I put into action my tried and true "stuff your feelings and smile" technique which had always been my default action when I felt that my words might cause me or someone else pain.

We drove back to our apartment complex in Cincinnati. The building was abuzz with students going in and out of the apartments, and I knew I would miss the camaraderie and the safety I felt among the residents. A few doors down from us, someone was throwing a party. The music and chatter gave me the courage to try and plant a tiny doubt regardingthe purchase of the ranch. Should we check a few more properties before buying this one? I asked My completely ignored my question as hespent a good portion of the night complaining about the noise from the party, making the ominous pronoucement "We will soon be surrounded by silence." I gave him a nervous laugh swallowing hard to avoid telling him that I felt "very uneasy" about our moving to the country in the middle of nowhere in Loveland, Ohio, to live in the creepy brother's ranch of disillusion and dead dreams.

I thought about broaching the subject several times but never got enough courage to present my ex with a well -thought argument free of hysterics that may have compelled my ex to "think before he bought". A week after seeing the ranch, we sat in the office of our third best friend in America, "The mortgage broker" from the Countrywide funding bank. I sat there telling myself,

"Now is too late to say anything; you're a chick, chick, chicken" That was one of the worst insults you could give a Brazilian. The purchase was now a done deal.

The mortgage broker was a jolly fellow, and he appeared to share a preference for a "dash" of color in his outfits, as did my ex. He wore a dark gray three-piece suit, the vest a bright red velour fitted tightly around his protruding stomach.

I told myself that everything would work out for the best. I looked at the red buttons that held the vest together. "This is the kind of faith I need," I thought to myself. I laughed out loud as I imagined the buttons finally giving way to the pressure from the broker's stomach and a wayward button hitting my ex in the eye, thus spectacularly interrupting the meeting.

My ex gave me the "cut it out look" as he pushed each document in my direction for me to sign, and I would pass it back to my ex, who signed it with a theatrical flourish.

We ended up with a small mountain of papers that gave us ownership of the ranch with the 33 acres.

I thought about our journey thus far and how we had accomplished owning a piece of the American dream and a Pontiac Grand Prix in mere months since arriving in the United States.

That thought failed to assuage my fears; instead, I recalled the failure of our first business venture, my ex trying his hand at being an art dealer. I shook my head to steer my thinking and perhaps our fate to a more positive and hopeful thought.

We left the office, and my ex drove us to his favorite restaurant, "The Ponderosa " for a dinner celebration.

I sat across the table watching my ex eating his sirloin steak; he would talk about his plans for the 33 acres between bites.

I had tried a spoon full of my soup and immediately had to reach for my glass of water. I drank in long gulps, wondering if the chef had accidentally dropped a pound of salt in the soup. Sodium appeared to be the main ingredient in all Ponderosa's dishes. I settled for desserts, only dinner, and coffee.

I looked at my ex and smiled. I had finally found the silver lining of moving to the ranch where we could have a place to hang the 57 paintings by the unknown Brazilian artists my ex hoped to bring out of anonymity.

We left Cincinnati and took occupancy in the ranch; even after so many years have passed, I still cannot call it "our home."

I knew that the ranch was where we would live, but it was also where I did not belong.

Nine months later, in the Spring of 1989, we would again sit in front of a broker, this time at the Fifth Third bank, where we signed the sale documents for the ranch and the 33 acres in Loveland, Ohio. We returned to an apartment in Cincinnati near the University, where we stayed put until my ex received his Master's degree.

# Chapter 10

## *The Gray Dog*

Back in Loveland ( ah, the irony of that name!), we unlocked the front door of our ranch and walked into the living room. The place smelled like a second-hand store.

I opened all the windows in the living room and the front door, leaving it open to "air out" the place.

I walked through the kitchen and opened the door that led to the garage. As the garage door slowly rolled up with a strident gear noise, I came face to face with a pair of eyes staring back at me.

The lights in the garage would not turn on. The light bulb must have gone out.

I tried to make out the dark shape of someone or something lying down on the cold cement, silently staring at me.

I called my ex over; the garage was now open, and a long-haired gray dog was lying on the garage floor, eerily still.

My ex and I looked at the dog; no one was moving for a few seconds.

My ex, who had never been a "dog person," shook his hand and stepped backward into the kitchen, saying, "No way, you deal with it; you like dogs." I stepped down to the garage, making kissy sounds.

The dog wagged his tail in approval; he looked about sixty or seventy pounds. The long coat of several shades of gray appeared matted in some places, and his ears stood alert.

A few feet from him, I sat on the ground and whistled softly, calling the dog to me. The dog stood with visible difficulty and slowly approached me.

I looked around the garage, realizing that the previous property owners had left that dog in the dark without food or water.

The dog was now very close; he buried his gray muzzle in my hand and leaned against me with a deep sigh, trusting my touch completely.

I petted his head and moved my fingers towards his back, his full coat soft with lots of white fur coming through as I continued to move my hands up and down his flank. The dog whimpered, sounding like he felt pain. I saw in horror dried blood coming from a small round wound on his side. I inspected the rest of his body and found several similar wounds, some still bleeding.

I started to feel my body heat up in anger, my eyes filled with tears as I ran inside to get the dog some water.

I cried, watching this gentle soul of a dog lapping the water anxiously; he was in obvious pain.

I went to look for the house phone; I dialed 911, not knowing who else to call. The police arrived quickly; I showed them the garage and told them of the sad surprise the ranch's previous owners had left for us.

The police officer kneeled by the dog, speaking to him softly, "It's ok old boy, you will be ok," while being careful to pet him on the head where there were no bullet wounds. I cried thinking about the cruel and malicious act of the brothers who knew we were taking possession of the ranch that day. I was shocked to see such cruelty towards a dog who had been part of the family for a long time judging by the dog's age. The officer took notes and asked if I would be willing to testify in this animal cruelty case.

"Of course," I answered, adding in my broken English, "I want to mean people to jail, ok?" The officer loaded the gray dog in their back seat, where they had set a blanket to keep the blood from his wounds from staining the seat.

They left, promising to call me back to let me know about the dog's condition and the cruelty case against the former owners of the ranch.

I sat outside for a long time, unwilling to cross the threshold of my front door. I looked around, not knowing how I would regain the resolve to continue our new journey that had just started so badly. My ex continued moving the boxes into the home, placing them in the living room carpet.

He would walk by me, asking if I was ok.

I wanted to scream, "No, I am not ok, I hate it here, and I want to go home!" I swallowed my sadness, knowing that becoming hysterical, which I could recognize as quickly becoming, wouldn't have been well received by my ex.

He appeared to have moved on emotionally, categorizing it in his brain as a "sad occurrence" that in no way tainted the experience he was now embarking.

I stood up and slowly walked toward our front door, hoping my second threshold crossing would magically transform the ranch into a peaceful, welcoming place free of sadness, cruelty, and trauma.

I entered the ranch with my eyes closed, ready for the miracle I had conjured in my mind. The musty smell still permeated the room and invaded my thoughts and the fantastic notion that my mental Abracadabra would work in dispelling the awful gut feeling I had.

I sat on one of the boxes and wiped the tears from my face.

My ex stood in front of me, one hand on his hip and another pointing towards our bedroom. I stood up, and as I mirrored his stance, I started singing, "I am a little teapot short and..." to bring some fun into our situation. My ex, who was never too impressed by my voice or PG humor, just stood there pointing to the room.

I nodded and walked towards the boxes marked "suite." I helped my ex carry the boxes to "our marital abode" where we would spend our nights embraced, sleeping blissfully, hopefully, maybe? The awful feeling that something was off remained long after emptying the contents of the last moving box.

# Chapter 11

## *Ohio Samba*

We worked side by side, and I emptied an entire Clorox bottle while cleaning the bathrooms and the kitchen.

I scrubbed the floors on my hands and knees as I tried to eliminate the house's musty, secondhand store smell. As I crawled around the bathroom scrubbing the tiles with a brush, I backed away into the carpet in our bedroom, and I felt the stickiness of the old shag carpet under my hands, which caused me to do a cat maneuver, jumping up on all fours back to the bathroom.

My ex found me still on my hands and knees, only my head picked out of the bathroom as I looked closely into the greasy and smelly shag carpet, trying to think of a way to clean it or send it back to hell where it belonged.

"E esto?" 'What is it?" yelled my ex; I told him that the carpet was "dis-gus- ting," carefully enunciating my new favorite and most used word at the ranch. He opened his arms, palms up in a gesture that asked, "what do you want me to do" while giving me his best " why did I marry a Brazilian martyrdom" look.

I stood up and slipped on my flip-flops; I walked into the carpet area and sat in our queen bed, where I had a notebook with a "to-do list" six pages long. I wrote, "have the carpets washed, preferably replaced or burned!"

I lay down for a moment inspecting the list, feeling the weariness of the heavy cleaning and scrubbing I had done trying to erase the past owner's presence that stubbornly lingered in the place.

That night, I dreamed about my childhood in Brazil.

I saw myself at the age of seven playing in the garden at the entrance of our building, surrounded by little critters, insects, and every creepy crawly imaginable that my mom would chase out of our home with her broom or the hand duster. She would complain bitterly about the inexistent cracks in our first-floor apartment walls that she kept scrupulously clean to the point of sterility. Wondering how little insects made their way into our home, never imagining that I would adopt them as my pets since I was not allowed to have a dog or a cat.

In my dream, I saw Bobbie, my parent's best friend's dog, a 20 lbs black poodle with an unhealthy obsession with balls. I loved Bobbie; she was a much-cherished dog of her owners who would kiss her on her shiny black nose, a practice that sent shivers down my mom's back as she would watch me attempt to do the same but was inevitably stopped by "the look" and a low growl from my mom who would whisper "don't you dare."

My mom was barely 5', weighed 115 lbs, and kept herself trimmed by never going for "seconds" during meals and engaging in a frenetic calisthenic routine that started when she would first wake up in the morning. She would kick the blankets off, activating the "air bicycle," riding the imaginary bicycle for a minute. She would then do the scissors exercises, crisscrossing her fully extended legs for another minute. She would then jump up from her bed, and with her arms outstretched at her sides, she would do fast circles, so fast that I worried that she might become airborne and need to be retrieved from the bedroom lights in the ceiling.

Fortunately, that never happened, and after generating

enough energy to light up a small village, my mom was ready for the day ahead.

My father was naturally slim and kept himself in shape by walking miles daily, ditching the car whenever possible, and working as a textile salesman on foot. His morning routine was directed first towards the fitness of his soul and, after the prayers, the maintenance of the health of everyone in the household.

He would sit by the window, wearing his prayer shawl, welcoming the first rays of sun with joy. His gaze up towards heaven, his eyes closed, he murmured the morning prayer "Mode Ani lefanecha…", a statement of gratitude to the Lord that had received his weary soul at night and had returned it, rested and renewed in the morning.

I would sit on his lap, playing with the fringes of the prayer shawl, and would be lulled to sleep by the soft murmuring of his words of gratitude. As soon as he was done, my father would remove his prayer shawl and phylacteries and carefully place them back in their velour case.

He would invariably clap his hand and say, "let's go," after offering a loud slap on his backside; his unique and humorous way to get himself geared for the day. That gesture always caused his laughter. He then would go to the kitchen to prepare platters of carefully cut-up fruits, cheese, jams, and delicious bread warm from the oven. He would place a whole banana for each of us next to a bowl of oatmeal for himself, my mom, and Geralda, the live-in maid; with that, his morning routine was complete.

Geralda, who had lived with us for twelve years, had neglected to inform my dad that she hated oatmeal. One day, Geralda came to my mom and told her that she was ready to leave her employment if she had to continue to eat the daily oatmeal. My father stopped making Geralda the oatmeal but added an orange to her plate, hoping it would maintain her health and vigor.

These dreams caused me to wake up hungry. I look around, trying to chase away the last wisps of my dream. I took a whiff of the cleaning agents I had used the night before and landed hard into the reality that I was living in the ranch Hope forgot to visit.

My ex was still asleep, so I stood up, slipped into my flip-flops, and planted a slap on my backside, hoping my father's method of getting himself ready for the day would also work for me. I decided I needed a second slap, which was witnessed by my ex, who had been startled awake by my first. I laughed at him nervously and hopped out of our bedroom, hoping my ex would think that the slapping and the hopping were part of a new exercise routine.

"I had never shared with my ex my father's good-humored routines. My ex had a tendency to dispense harsh judgment at any sign of what he called "childish and foolish behavior."

I walked into our kitchen and located the coffee maker and the coffee in the open box on the counter. I opened the refrigerator, where I found a small milk bottle. I made a mental note about buying groceries. I leaned on the counter, sipping my coffee. My ex walked into the kitchen.

I handed him his mug, and he held it with both hands and lifted it to his lips, finishing the brew in two gulps. My ex and I were still unaccustomed to drinking coffee from a big mug that would be used for soup in Brazil. Coffee in Brazil is served in tiny cups in Brazil all day long. The dark, full-of-flavor beverage has enough caffeine to energize your mind and body in seconds.

Mornings in Brazil bring you out of sleep at first light, which has already awakened every bird in the city as they go about their business, singing and chirping in an incessant salute to the morning sun.

The smell of coffee wafts in the air, with its rich and luscious aroma sneaking into your nostrils, causing the eyes to pop open as the brain anticipates the first dose of caffeine of the day. The birds are joined by the sounds of the city coming alive, with music being the last component that brings a Brazilian out of sleep.

Despite Brazil's love (bordering on obsession) for everything American, Samba is still the music that nurtures one and all, rich or poor, old or young, whose body becomes electric and moves to even the faintest sounds of the irresistible Samba.

Samba has a mixture of tambourines, drums, agogo bells, surdos, ganzas, cuica, timbals, pandeiros, and repiniques. 'Many instruments are fashioned from the remnants of trees, seeds, fibers, and animal hides.

The African origins of Samba tell their story of slavery and pain, which is felt most poignant in the cuica sound, an instrument that sounds like a scream, a profound lament that is felt deep in your soul. The drums and tambourines emerge from within the melody, growing in a crescendo accompanied by the heartbeat of the Samba dancer.

Samba emerged from the enslaved Africans hiding in the "quilombo," "the war camp" that served as a refuge where they would meet at night to tell stories from their land, so no one would forget their heritage as they waited for freedom.

They sang and danced, their bodies glistening with sweat and pain. The old would tell stories filled with longing for their home, so far away. They made instruments from hollowed tree trunks and rosined strings, carefully peeled from the tree barks.

The old and the young united in spirit through their songs and rhythms, their hearts beating as one as they raised their voices, despair intertwined with Hope, longing for their freedom.

Samba unites Brazilians of all colors and backgrounds during the three days of Carnaval when paupers are indistinguishable from the rich as they dance their pains and glories for three days in February.

With those thoughts and memories in mind, I retrieved my "boombox" radio and cassette player" from one of the cardboard boxes. I placed "Samba's greatest hits" in the cassette and turned the volume way up; we were in the middle of nowhere, surrounded by silence; the only noise complaints would have been from the unseen creatures that lived in the trees.

The beat of a solo drum, the "batuque," leads slowly to the sudden appearance of hundreds of drums of all sizes in an explosion of sound that penetrates the body, eliciting an irresistible desire to move every limb and body part in the Samba rhythms.

I joined my favorite singer Clara Nunes as she sang, "O canto de tres raças" or "The chant of three races" my feet moved quickly, small steps forward, small steps back. My hips seemingly disengaged from my waist, free to gyrate and sway from side to side. My ex smiled; he tried his version of a samba step. Together, we emptied the boxes in our new home as we blended our belongings, memories, and dreams of a bright future inside the dreary ranch in Loveland, Ohio.

# Chapter 12

## *Love In The Listing Ship*

The weekend flew by. We had arranged and rearranged the furniture and the little knick knacks that had emerged intact from the boxes. We had failed to make the living room into a cozy area and the bedroom suite less... dismal. We agreed that the house had an awkward layout, and I hoped its weird energy would eventually turn bright and light instead of funky and dreary.

I missed the little apartment in Cincinnati and the sound of other humans, busy with their own lives in the apartment complex, which gave me a sense of safety. The silence in the ranch had a hollow feel; like all the other sounds had felt oppressed and decided to up and leave.

I dreaded Mondays since my ex had to return to the University in Cincinnati, leaving me to spend the day alone.

I would drive 45 minutes to drop him off and pick him up. The Pontiac Grand Prix, our only transportation, would be clocking many miles during the year that we lived...er... survived in Loveland.

I had stocked our cars with my favorite cassette tapes from Samba to John Denver to Yiddish songs. I believed my voice to be stunning while singing in the car and the shower. Incredibly, my ex did not share my enthusiasm or belief in the extraordinary quality of my singing voice. For this reason, I was looking forward to dropping Mr. Critic at the University so I could finally have the chance to be in the driver's seat of our Pontiac Grand Prix and sing to my heart's content.

My ex, having been born and raised in Argentina, where the roles assignments in marriage were clear and immutable: Men drive; if men are not there, then women drive; women cook; if women manage to escape, then men order out until he finds another woman to cook for him. Laundry, dishes, cleaning, decorating...also falls under the chapter "what men don't do" in the centuries-old "Guide to being the men," a popular publication in Latin America.

In our home in Brazil; my father was active in the household front and in their business. The discussion of gender roles never came up in our home.

My mom minded the clothing store they owned in the Bom Retiro neighborhood. My father would spend the day visiting the textile factories he represented and return in the late afternoon to the clothing store to help my mom close it up for the day.

My parents functioned like a single organism in perfect harmony with the sum of its parts. They had met each other aboard the "Listing ship."

The vessel named *Latrun* (formerly known as *San Dimitrio*) was barely seaworthy and listed sharply to one side. The ship's captain, a fellow that was either suicidal or very brave, would direct a portion of the 1,275 transported Holocaust survivors to stand in groups on one side of the ship to straighten the ramshackle ship temporarily. The survivors had organized themselves in groups to work in the kitchen and other maintenance duties necessary to keep the boat afloat.

The bleary-eyed, traumatized survivors sat in the dining hall area, leaning on each other, some bundled up in blankets, their emaciated bodies unable to produce heat. They were too sick to move, and it was unclear if they would survive the journey.

They waited for the meals prepared by the survivors working as the kitchen crew. They found out that the boat's water was contaminated due to the boat listing too close to the ocean water. They had to boil buckets and buckets of water from the ship's water until they could put together a soup for the passengers and crew.

My father was in charge of bringing the empty bowls of soup back to the kitchen from the dining hall to continue distributing the life-saving nourishment to all aboard. My father approached the table where my mother sat, slowly eating her soup, her arm protectively cradling the bowl, the years of hunger and starvation still clinging to her mind and body.

My father finished loading the bowls in a cart, and he looked towards my mom, a diminutive figure, her long locks of black hair picking out from the blanket bundled around her body. Their eyes met; my father's cerulean blue eyes twinkling with kindness, met my mom's dark eyes; she brought her arm closer to the bowl, and she started at him in defiance she ate slowly each bite of food bringing her relief from starvation.

My father told us the story of the moment he fell in love with my mother. He saw her indomitable spirit, drive, and courage in that fiery stare. My mother would never tire of hearing their story; she would rest her head on my father's shoulder while he told it. She would look at him cupping his face with her hands, planting a kiss on his nose, and playfully biting it as my father would dramatically hold his nose, pretending to pluck the bitten piece and showing it to us in his version of "I got your nose."

My parents' love for each other had an intense quality that would sometimes exclude others. They would turn to each other in difficult times, merging into one that possessed all the necessary skills to defeat the problem. Their bond was forged in their shared experience of survival against all odds.

My father supported my mother's many interests, including

baking. Her cakes would inevitably fail to rise; their thin appearance gained the name "postal cakes" as it was possible to send the chewy concoction by mail in case anyone was interested in trying them. My father, forever the optimist, full of love for my mother, was the only one who would eat her deflated creation.

He would spend at least ten minutes chewing one piece, saying, "Yummm, this one is your best," while his jaw would make a clicking sound as he ground his piece of cake while looking lovingly at my smiling mother. Later in life, my father suffered from TMJ. Most likely due to the overuse of his jaws while eating my mom's baked goods.

I looked at my ex as I recalled my parents' love and devotion towards each other. We had been married for less than a year at that time. My ex looked back at me, sensing that he was being watched. I looked deeply into his green eyes, hoping that my dark eyes would communicate my feelings and that we would find the same enduring love in each other's gaze. My ex looked at me quizzically, and after a few seconds, he asked me, "Are you feeling all right?

I sighed and thought that I should have winked at him mid-gaze, and perhaps that would have done the trick. I looked at my ex, who now had the "there she goes again " expression, which brought me back to reality.

I got up and told him I was getting ready for bed. I entered our bedroom suite, the ceiling's harsh light illuminating the drab room. I walked into the bathroom suite for my nightly shower. I closed the shower curtains, closing my eyes as the warm water washed away the tiredness of the last few days. I decided to give my marriage and the ranch a hefty dose of TLC. I felt invigorated. I decided to go shopping the next day after dropping off my ex at the University.

I would buy lovely curtains, side tables, and beautiful bedside lamps to bring a less harsh glow to the room. A warm and cozy light, I decided, would help me ease into my sleep, giving me rest that was unperturbed by dreams of being back home.

The feeling that something deeply unsettling continued to inhabit the ranch remained in my gut, unabated. My ex entered the bedroom and joined me in bed after turning off the lights; his breathing became steady within minutes as he drifted off to sleep.

I kept whispering to myself, "go to sleep." I finally fell asleep into a dreamless and silent vacuum akin to the oppressive silence of the ranch.

# Chapter 13

## *Sorry, Ma'am, We Had To Deploy An Aircraft...*

My ex drove to the University on College hill neighborhood in Cincinnati on Monday morning bright and early. I quickly moved to the driver's seat of our superb American-made vehicle, our Night Blue Pontiac Grand Prix.

I felt inspired by the Grand Prix name and my sudden freedom.

After waving to my ex, I departed the parking lot; the tires let out a squeal as I pressed hard on the gas pedal, eager to experience the joys of driving an automatic transmission car.

I had consulted the map of Cincinnati and was driving on Clifton avenue. The year was 1988, and we were at least ten years away from the most significant American invention in history, the "Google" search engine.

I had the handy dandy city map, which forced me to develop my navigation skills, and when I got lost, which happened to me quite often, I would engage in the social dynamic of asking for directions.

My English fluency was still in the budding phase; my accent and the peculiar way that Brazilians have to finish any word that ends in a consonant by adding an "I" that sounds like "e" confused the individuals who were nice enough to give me directions.

I would often face a bewildered stare from Scotee, our usual server at the local diner, whom I would ask for a "cupy" of coffee, "a glassy" of water, and a "dishi" to split up my "foody" with my ex.

Scott would always respond with a broad smile, bringing us anything he could decipher between my ex's and my quasi-English and our abundance of hand gestures.

Having to ask for directions while having a cultural speech impediment meant that my outings would take a bit longer, as I would try several pronunciations of the same word. Fortunately, America is filled with generous and patient gas station attendants who would eventually understand what I was asking and answer in a loud voice as if my lack of fluency in English was also a sign of hearing loss.

After dropping off my ex, I got off on the correct exit on the Highway after spotting the sign for Northgate Mall located on mall road; how convenient and clever, I thought to myself in my ongoing love affair with everything American.

I drove into the enormous parking lot, choosing a spot near the entrance; I was ready for my first real solo Mall experience.

In Brazil, the Shopping Center Iguatemi was a replica of an American Mall, only much smaller. I joined the shoppers, hurriedly entering the numerous stores and exiting with several shopping bags, their faces showing the expressions of someone who had just conquered a war. I looked at the racks of merchandising with a "Sale" sign.

I wondered what the reason was for announcing that the items were for sale. Why else would they have it in a store? That day marked my discovery of the "sales rack," giving me a new understanding of the conquest smile as the shoppers hurried out of the stores before the store owner had a chance to change their minds. The discovery had a positive impact on our wallet and a negative one on our marriage.

My ex was obsessed with the endless possibilities in attire since discovering "the sale's rack." His love for fashion would have us shopping for hours. He would hold each garment he had pulled off the rack and stare at it with the concentration and pause of a judge who had to consider someone's life or death. I would feign excitement as he entered the dressing room, arms filled with garments selected to be tried on.

The second step in my ex's process involved me standing in the tiny dressing room, the mirrors reflecting my ex's approval or rejection of the dozens of outfits he would try on. I would try to match his excitement over a particular outfit until his expression would change to disapproval, and the garment would be discarded.

I was a bit slow in accompanying my ex's clothes selection, and I would, at times, erroneously give him the thumbs up to a rejected item causing him to give me an indignant look as if he was witnessing a grave character flaw.

I realized my opinion would never match his because I was happy with jeans and T-shirts, flannel shirts, and Carhartt jackets in the Winter. A style that would become mytrademark that I called my "Lumberjack chic" style.

I finished shopping and gathered my purchases, placing them in the car's back seat. I consulted the map for the best way back to Loveland and the ranch. I quickly found the way to the I-71 Highway used by my ex to drive us to the University and back to Loveland.

I merged into the light traffic of midday. I looked at the speed limit sign; 70 was the limit. I acknowledge it fully, intending to obey it.

I cranked the radio cassette to "blaring" and sang the song it played. The Pontiac Grand Prix quietly accelerated to the speed limit; I thought, "Very good, I will maintain this speed."

I relaxed into my seat, enjoying the ease of driving an automatic transmission. I held the steering wheel with one hand while using my right hand to conduct the fabulous Beethoven 7th symphony for piano and orchestra now playing.

I had pulled up all my windows for better sound and the chill in the air. I noticed as I drove that everyone driving on the Highway let me pass them. "How kind," I thought to myself, giving each driver a smile and a wave and then returning to conducting the symphony orchestra.

I drove county to county, enjoying the speed, the driving, and the courtesy American drivers showed. Suddenly, I saw a policeman's car's red and blue lights flashing behind me. In addition I could hear a helicopter fast approaching, flying lower and lower while matching my speed. The pilot was now visible, his hand making a "slowdown" gesture.

I still thought I was in the way, and the policeman was trying to pass me on his way to fight crime. I opened the window and stuck my arm out, making a "pass me" sign with my hand. The policeman continued behind me, imprudently close to the back of my Pontiac Grand Prix.

I suddenly heard a voice coming through a megaphone, "Lady, stop the car!" I started to consider the possibility that the policeman behind me was telling ME to stop. "Oh my goodness, I am the lady!" I looked in the rearview mirror and through the windshield, seeing no other car driving other than the cars driving on the other side of the median.

I slowly stopped the car at the side of the highway. I wondered if I should follow the traffic stop protocol used in Brazil. I decided that I should.

In Brazil, if a cop stops you, you are expected to turn off the ignition and exit the car to greet the police officer and show them that you are not carrying firearms or weapons.

I was full of confidence as I exited the car, giving the policeman my best smile as I walked towards him. To my surprise, the policeman stood behind his opened door and yelled, "Stop." I had started feeling uneasy at that point, thinking something was wrong.

The policeman, still standing behind his open door, told me to put my arms up and "Keep turning around until I tell you to stop." He then instructed me to stay standing and to place my hands on the hood of my Pontiac Grand Prix.

I could feel the tears start to well in my eyes; a second later, I cried full-on. I imagined myself wearing a striped jumpsuit, having my first experience in an American prison.

The police officer approached me and told me to calm down; he looked at me up and down, visually confirming my absence of guns as he waited for my tears to stop. I wore jeans and a T-shirt in the warmth of my car's great heater. I was now chilled with fear combined with the wind and the rapidly descending temperature.

The policeman asked me to turn around in a calm tone. I followed his prompt and, in between tears, hiccups, and blowing my nose on a handkerchief handed to me by the policeman, I started to calm down.

He asked me for my ID and proof of insurance. I was able to give him my driver's license and my passport as well as the yellow paper given to us by our friend, the car salesman who had explained that we "had" to have insurance, another Novel idea for both myself and my ex. I had followed his advice and kept all the documents together in the glove compartment.

I thought about how the policeman and I would soon share a hearty laughter, about how he had mistakenly taken me for a wanted criminal. He would then give me back my documents, and "all will be forgiven" as we exchanged apologies, and he would become my third best friend in America.

The policeman inspected the documents as he sat in his car, talking on a two-way radio. I could see his smile as he walked back, giving me the documents and an extra piece of paper that read "traffic violation" in bold letters. The reality set in that "all was not forgotten" as he gave me a ticket. He listened to my pleas to reconsider issuing me a ticket. He patiently listened as I told him about my ex, who was only slightly less grumpy than Henry VIII.

He smiled again as he explained he could not "let it go with just a warning" because "an aircraft had to be deployed" in the pursuit.

He further explained that he would "get in trouble" if he did not issue me a ticket after clocking my driving speed to over 90 miles.

I was dumbfounded and a little impressed by the Pontiac Grand Prix's smooth ride. I shared with this infinitely patient officer that this was my first experience driving a car with automatic transmission and my first ever speeding ticket.

I still hoped to avoid a ticket and my ex's wrath. I was still holding the ticket and the officer appeared eager to leave; he touched the side of his police hat and wished me "a great rest of my day." He walked back to his police unit, reminding me of the speed limit and telling me to "slow down." My eyes got misty with emotion as I solemnly told him, "I promise," while weighing the pros and cons of singing the few words of the National Anthem to the officer as further proof of my sincerity and devotion to America.

The policeman, most likely sensing an awkward moment was about to occur, said goodbye and left.

The helicopter had long been gone, back to where police helicopters go after a speed chase.

I drove home slowly, carefully checking the dashboard, maintaining a speed between 65 and 70.

I arrived on the ranch safely. I walked in and had a glass of sugared water, a remedy for frazzled nerves in Brazil. With great resolve, I retrieved the shopping bags from the car and started preparing a delicious meal. I planned to serve it to my ex once we returned to the ranch after I picked him up from the University. I would ask about his day as he drove us back to the ranch, my ex would sit in the driver's seat, and for once, I would be relieved to have him drive us.

I would tell him about the 62 dollar speeding ticket after the meal or maybe after he enjoyed a good night's rest...or two nights' rest. I imagined myself telling my ex about the speeding ticket as I casually mentioned the word "aircraft" while giving him my "can you imagine!"

# Chapter 14

---

## *Lawn And Order*

**M**y ex had been surprisingly calm about the speeding ticket, and we could laugh about the incident after I pinky-promised never to speed again.

The weekend started with my ex and I eating breakfast and drinking coffee. My ex read the News section of the local newspaper while I concentrated on the Classifieds session, still looking for a puppy. At that point, I had already learned that using the word "housebroken" in a pet classified ad wasn't an announcement of the sad "break up in the pet's home" or impending divorce of their owners' marriage.

That knowledge helped me look for a puppy without deciding between a dog from a broken home or a happy home.

That Sunday, I saw an ad for a schnauzer puppy; Queenie had been the last one of the litter, a sign, I thought as I sat across from my ex on that leisurely Sunday morning.

I had grown up in an environment filled with tales of divine providence and deep faith. My parents' survival had been nothing short of a miracle. Their families and friends were annihilated for no reason other than a man's evil madness and thirst for power and hatred for those he feared. Some had followed him blindly detaching from the shared human condition, believing themselves to be the "superior race".

My mother had survived, with her older sister, the destruction of the Warsaw Ghetto, their internment in Majdanek, and the work at the Hassag ammunition factory. My mother's keen intelligence and quick wit saved her many times as she wrote popular songs filled with hope and humor in a place surrounded by death.

My father had survived five different death camps, including Buchenwald, where he would mesmerize the other prisoners with his sweet nature, faith, and kindness in a place where forgetting your humanity was expected.

Brazil was uniquely suited to those whose hearts were filled with fear. The good-natured people of Brazil and the warm weather acted as a balsam to my parents' souls.

Brazilians are profoundly spiritual and accepting of all faiths, creating an amalgam of creeds and religious practices intertwined in the history of those that immigrated to Brazil, those who were brought as slaves, and the Brazilian natives, the beautiful people of the forests. The combination of different religions and folklore existed in an atmosphere of acceptance and curiosity.

> Brazilians of all faiths are known for adopting practices that are not part of their religion but are accepted as a "let's do it just in case," so as not to incur the disfavor of an entity from a different religion.

One such custom is the new year's celebration for Yemanja, the ocean goddess. All participants wear white and go to the beach, where music plays all night long; the ocean waters are lit with candles and gift offerings from the believers.

My parents never threw anything on the ocean as gifts or lit any candles; they did wear white; in fact, we all did, and we walked on the sand near the water's edge, saying high to friends, families, and neighbors who had joined in the festivities year after year.

Growing up in such an intense spiritual atmosphere created in me a continuous dance between the rational and the mystical that, in my opinion, offered a more significant advantage since everything and anything was possible in the supernatural and the divine.

Since I tended to keep my mind open to almost everything that was not illegal, blasphemous, cruel, or a lie, I struggled to create a healthy balance between "a need" and a "want." "What if a want is truly a sign that I needed it"? I would spend hours philosophically considering my options until I usually opted for the "want."

Queenie, the miniature Schnauzer, was "a want" for sure, but she was also a "need " due to the many hours I had to spend alone on the ranch. Queenie was the last pup in the litter to find a home, which was a sure sign that she and I had been divinely brought together into each other's life.

With all the bases covered and a quick phone call for directions, we left to retrieve our "meant-to- be" puppy, who would be undoubtedly happy to be finally in the arms of her rightful owners.

We drove home with a fuzzy gray ball of energy, she had floppy little ears and a shiny black nose surrounded by the gray fuzz.

Queenie had more fuzz around her pink mouth and licked me furiously, ecstatic to be in my arms. Queenie was not only heaven-sent but also a "holy terror."Miniature Schnauzers belonged to the terror's lineage that produced dogs called "terrors," such as the Jack Russel and Yorkshire "terrors."

Queenie was lovely and cuddly, which was all a ruse to distract us from the fact that our little furry "daughter" was independent and strong-willed with very little care about where she would relieve herself in the house or the perils of the woods surrounding the ranch.

She would follow us outside obediently five times a day; potty training was imperative as she had chosen the shaggy carpet in our bedroom as her restroom for a little while. She did potty train in two weeks, to everyone's relief, including Queenie's, who would jump at my ex's voice, yelling, "No, no."

Queenie loved the woods around the ranch; she would start smelling the ground near us, slowly gaining distance until suddenly, she would stand immobile for a few seconds as she smelled the air before engaging her back legs into running in place as seen in cartoons.

My ex would turn around and walk straight home, grumbling she was "your problem," annoyed at Queenie's lack of common sense and self-preservation since he was sure "something" could end up eating our sweet "daughter."

I shared his concern and would run after Queenie, yelling her name and doing the opposite of what is required to teach a dog recall. The grass grew around us at an alarming pace. Queenie became less and less visible during our morning and afternoon chase sessions.

Queenie must have taken my screeching as my own "barking style" and a sign of approval of her leadership skills. Finally, Queenie was fitted with a collar and a leash.

Queenie's response to this sudden lack of freedom was to give several alligators "death rolls," stopping only to retrieve the treats that were sold to us at the pet store with the leash and the collar, as well as a book on "how to train a dog."

Queenie learned that walks meant being on a leash, and she would walk by my side, matching my steps.

The grass around us continued to grow until we became surrounded by tall grass that reached above our knees. The growing grass became our daily topic of discussion on tackling the issue that we "city folk" did not consider when purchasing a country home.

My ex and I had grown up in a sea of asphalt and cement, surrounded by skyscrapers, where the landscape always seemed to remain the same. The grass in our building was always kept short by some invisible powers outside our knowledge or awareness.

We had apparently missed that our parents would pay maintenance fees to enjoy a carefully designed and maintained landscape. We were clueless about being responsible for anything other than what was inside a house. There was no thought or consideration given to the fact that we were leaving the well-maintained building complex near the University that, just like in our childhood homes, the grass never grew, and the landscape remained the same.

How on earth did we miss that country living meant plants and plants left to their own devices would grow a lot?

Now my ex and I would stand in the doorway, trying to find the path we had managed to make as we stepped on the tall weeds, bending them as we walked to our car, which was still somewhat visible as it sat at the gravel entrance to the property.

We search the newspaper classifieds for landscaping companies. We had a few landscapers show up, and they would invariably laugh and say, "Wow, what happened here?" Our command of the English language was still far from great, causing us to take their question literally. "Oh my goodness!" we would tell each other, "They don't know HOW this happened?" That question made us doubt their competence if they, like us, had "missed the biology class" on how plants grow.

We eventually learned colloquialisms and stopped answering questions in the literal sense. One of the landscapes refused to do the job, saying that a large tractor would be needed in "this massive job" while pointing to the tall grass surrounding the ranch, several hundred feet in all directions, including what used to be the "backyard" which extended to the 33 acres of trees.

The other landscaper gave us a paper with the itemized list that included the rental of a tractor and the final cost of 2000 dollars and 65 dollars for weekly maintenance and snow removal for the Winter.

My ex stared at the piece of paper, his bottom lip trembling as he read and reread the landscaper's quote.

I sensed that the landscaper was only minutes away from witnessing a scene from the *I Love Lucy* sitcom as my ex summoned his internal "Ricky Ricardo," complete with a flurry of hand gestures and a heavy Spanish accent.

I hurriedly thanked the landscaper and told him we would call him after discussing his proposal. He walked towards his truck, telling us before departing, "Call me soon, or you will never find your way out." His laugh now faded as he drove away.

My ex was still in full-on "pre-explosion" mode, the vapor of his breath visible in the chilly air, surrounding his head in a halo of frustration. The expletives came with many frenetic arms gestures and "air punching".

I followed him to the ranch silently; he sat in the kitchen, still talking a mile a minute while I prepared him a cup of coffee while trying to remember if we had any sedatives at home. I hoped that the coffee and pastries were enough to regulate his mood. My ex munched on the pastries, speaking about the outrageous price given to us to "just cut plants!"

He stopped talking and chewing for a moment, suddenly still.

I thought I saw a lightbulb suddenly appear at the top of his head with a "ding" sound as my ex proclaimed to have found a solution. He held his index finger in the air and he instructed me to call rental gardening stores on Monday first thing in the morning. He announced that he would "do the job himself," just as The "early Americans" had done in the Wild West.

My ex finished his speech by sounding poetic, "They conquered the land and made it theirs." My ex's eyes were excited as he imagined himself triumphant, riding a tractor for the first time in his life as the fearless land owner he thought he was. He would bring order to the chaotic landscape that seemed to grow each second it remained rooted to the ground. I nodded enthusiastically, relieved and proud to see his frustration give way to a plan.

My ex continued to explain to me his plan that would culminate in a shopping trip for a lawn mower of our own to keep the "the damned grass short"! He slapped his forehead in a humorous gesture: "How didn't I think of that."

The following day I returned to the ranch after dropping off my ex's University, ready to put my ex's plan into motion. I picked up the yellow pages, where I would find a "home, farm, and garden" rental store. Luckily they had the tractor we needed with the attached accessories, powerful enough to cut down the "Amazon forest," the store clerk quipped. He saluted my Brazilian heritage after trying unsuccessfully to match my accent to my country of origin.

The tractor would be delivered on Saturday early morning, when my brave ex would conquer our wild land, emerging victorious. "Boy, we are getting so melodramatic," I told myself, thinking about how stressful country living was.

I imagined my ex stepping down from the tractor after finishing the job, leisurely chewing on a blade of grass, a subtle warning to the grass growing around us that a new "sheriff" was in town.

"Lawn and order" will be restored in the town of Loveland in Goshen Township, Ohio. I could hear the twang of the western melodies that played in the background of the Western-themed movies of my childhood.

# Chapter 15

## *Overalls In Tall Grass*

The week went by with rain and a thunderstorm, and the weather was getting progressively cold. I highly anticipated the potential snow that would arrive in a few weeks. I would let the fluffy white flakes gather in my mouth, tasting my first bit of snow, marveling at the fragility of snowflakes as they would come down in solid form, only to melt in my tongue in a matter of seconds.

Thinking about snow brought me back to the problem at hand.

We had learned from the person at the landscape rental place that "we would have a mess" on our hands if the snow arrived before we had cut the grass.

The rains had encouraged the grass to grow even taller. Saturday morning arrived, and at 8:00 AM sharp, I heard some banging and loud voices outside the ranch. I couldn't see outside the window as the landscape reached higher than our windows in a sea of yellow/green grass, half dry but still growing as if it was participating in a "who is the tallest" grass competition.

I walked outside, stopping to decide which path to take. We walked daily back and forth from the car parked in the gravel to our doorstep, the flattened grass indicating a reliable way to go through the reeds until they sprung back up to their original place.

I could hear the loud voices of the delivery men; I followed the sounds and emerged from the grass, catching them by surprise with my "howdy partner" greeting.

Most of my English lessons had come from watching old Western movies and Johnny Carson, who provided me with fun nightly classes as I sat on the couch next to my ex.

I would wait for the announcer to hurry up and finish the endless "is" between "here" and "Johnny," fidgeting on the couch looking for the most comfortable spot; my frequent change in position would inevitably cause my ex to shout, "Basta, caramba!"

My ex enjoyed Western movies; he would parrot his favorite actor, Clint Eastwood, by saying "make my day" interchangeably during marital conflict or lovemaking.

In my early days as an English speaker, I believed that a well-placed, colloquially specific word in our geographical location would convey to the locals that I cared about their culture, language, and customs.

I hoped that my "Howdy partner" greeting would be seen as a sign of solid confidence in my ranching skills, leading them to assume that the wild state of the landscape had been an "agricultural experiment" and not ignorance of basic lawn care.

My ex and I finally realized that owning a lawnmower would have prevented this ordeal. I knew I did not fool the nice delivery man into believing that I was comfortable with the state of the property as I emerged from the "jungle" of grass and weeds, wearing some of them, as they stuck to my long hair like a spiky crown.

I shook hands with the nice delivery men as I casually removed the weeds from my head.

The man closest to me initiated the dialogue, speaking rapidly, his words heavy with a Midwest accent; he walked towards the flatbed truck, beckoning me to follow him. The colossal tractor was intimidating; I had not imagined its size when I ordered from the rental store. The idea that my ex could operate this heavy machine safely felt preposterous as I recalled his struggles with a supermarket cart that kept veering to the right during one of our shopping trips.

The delivery driver seemed to be in a hurry; he spoke to me very fast, stopping between his fast speech to look at me and ask ok? I would nod "yes" to every question. He jumped on the tractor's cabin, offering me his hand; he lifted me onto the truck with ease, and I looked down at the ground, which looked so far away.

He proceeded to show me the gear shift and the buttons on the panels. I fell silent as he moved to show me the pedals. There were five of them; why so many? I thought I was about to ask the question but decided against it as I thought about my English fluency, or lack thereof, in this case.

Attempting to learn how to operate heavy machinery while speaking rudimentary English learned from TV was slowly bringing me to the realization that my ex's idea to rent a truck and cut the jungle himself may not be the best course of action.

I tried to understand the instructions and commit them to memory. I knew it was too late to change our minds; my ex was still in bed, and I had been tasked to learn tractor driving well enough to later transmit the knowledge to him, so he could sleep late.

My ex had dismissed my suggestion that we take turns working with the tractor. "This is not a woman's job," he said, sighing dramatically. "This is a man's job," he affirmed. His masculinity would have endowed him genetically in all matters related to heavy labor, including driving a tractor. I stopped thinking of the possible disastrous outcomes. I would follow through with our money-saving option by learning from the man now seated on the tractor.

I focused on gaining knowledge by watching the delivery man.

He told me, "Hang on," as he confidently turned it on and off, blades up, blades down, driving a few feet and stopping giving me the thumbs up. I was feeling a bit dizzy from all the head nodding and from holding my full attention to the instructions given to me.

The continuous focus has always been a monumental task for my brain. My thoughts would bounce free, from topic to topic; I was eternally entertained by life and novelty; each learning opportunity was irresistible. The driver asked me, "Ok?" one last time before telling me they would return to collect the tractor on Monday morning. They climbed into their truck and waved goodbye as they drove away.

I sighed deeply as my previous gut feelings about the ranch returned to me in full force. I walked back, beating down the reeds with my arms as I tried to find the front door. I walked in, and Queenie, the Terror, greeted me excitedly, ready for her morning walk.

I yelled for my ex, who was still in bed, telling him, "we have the tractor"! I clicked on the leash on Queenie's collar, and we both walked out, Queenie staying right behind me as I cleared a path for her. We eventually found our way to the gravel; Queenie snuffled and snorted loudly, carefully inspecting the areas she deemed possible sites for her daily "deposits." After a lot of circling, she finally settled for the spot near the tree line.

I walked back carrying Queenie in my arms, enjoying our morning cuddle. I put her down inside and prepared Queenie's breakfast and our own. I entered our bedroom suite; the olive-green shag carpet muffled the sounds of my steps. I called my ex softly; there was no movement in the bed.

I pounced on him like a cat, playfully tousling his hair, his face resting on the pillow. I gave him lots of noisy kisses as I tried to pull him out of whatever dream he was having. He finally stirred and looked up at me, one eyebrow up, his way of communicating displeasure. I smiled at him, ignoring the scowl.

He disliked waking up by anyone other than his circadian

rhythm. "The tractor, the tractor is here," giving my ex my best "Tattoo" from the *Fantasy Island* interpretation. My ex bolted from the bed; he asked me to wait for him in the kitchen as he "got ready." That was an unusual request from my ex, who would require my presence to help him decide what to wear from his extensive wardrobe.

I waited impatiently for his appearance in our kitchen and slowly drank my coffee while eyeing theclosed door to our bedroom from where my ex would soon emerge.

I was soon distracted by an interesting article in our local paper about a new movie theater in our area when suddenly I heard my ex shouting, "Tadaa." His arms were outstretched, and he danced, finishing his presentation with a loud "yeehaa" after slapping himself on his tight.

I was speechless. My ex stood in the middle of the living room, posing with his hands on his waist, wearing brand new jeans overalls, a flannel shirt neatly tucked in the overall pants, a red handkerchief tied around his neck, and pointy cowboy boots that completed the ensemble.

My ex had transformed himself into a real-life farmer with a cowboy flavor, thanks to the brown boots where he had tucked his pants legs. He sat down and drank his coffee, munching on buttered toast and talking about his plan to deal with our over-grown landscape at once.

I was still mesmerized by his outfit; he seemed a bit uncom-fortable walking in his boots as he stopped pulling them off and putting them back on while using me as support to prevent himself from stepping on the grass wearing his socks. We reached the tractor, and I could see my ex's concern as he sized up the machine.

We climbed onto the cabin, and I showed the steps necessary to turn on the tractor and maneuver it while keeping the blades up until reaching the tall grass. My ex seemed comfortable with my instructions; he was concerned just as I had been with the number of pedals. I remembered the accelerator, gear, and brake pedals; I had only a faint recollection of the utility of the other two pedals.

My ex turned on the tractor, and it roared to life. He told me to wait for him inside because he felt that "he had it under control" and would finish the entire job "in no time." We kissed as if he was going to war. I jumped off the tractor, waving him goodbye, eyes misty at my ex's courage and drive.

I closed our door and stood by the window, hoping very soon to see my ex riding the tractor over the tall weeds that blocked my view. About three minutes later, my ex opened the front door, closed it, and locked it. My ex's eyes were huge; his breathing labored from running from "two real snakes," in panic, telling me how he had seen them emerge from the patch of grass, causing him to "run for his life." "I am not going out there," he yelled. "I love my life, you know."

He had removed his boots and the handkerchief from his neck, using it to dry off the sweat from his face. He got himself a glass of water, and with a loud "ugh," he settled on the couch, sipping from the glass while murmuring, "Snakes, they were after me." I knew better than to question this hypothesis as he appeared to be very close to a hysterical fit. We had paid almost 400 dollars for the tractor rental.

The weeds were getting higher by the minute, and hiring professional landscapers would have cost us their quote, 2,000 dollars plus the 400 dollars of the rental, and we still had to buy a lawnmower.

I decided to give the tractor a try myself; my ex, still shaken from the experience, told me, "Suit yourself; you won't be able to do it, you will see."

The words "you won't be able" had always fueled my resolve.

I wore my jeans and a warm jacket; I put on a hat gathering my long hair to keep it away from the snakes, just in case they were jumping snakes. In Brazil, snakes were common even in my town's asphalt jungle of São Paulo. I was ready for the tractor.

I left my ex on the couch holding Queenie the front door was left unlocked, as I was sure that it was highly unlikely that a snake would break into a home despite my ex's assertion of that possibility, after all how could they with no arms or legs, for once, I was the one making a whole lot of sense I walked quickly to the tractor, keeping my eyes on the ground. I had a steak knife in my jacket pocket, just in case.

I sat on the tractor and turned it on, engaging into first gear, and there I went. I found driving the tractor pretty easy; I had only driven stick-shift cars, so I quickly managed to maneuver the behemoth over the grass thinking this was "not bad."

After driving for a little while to really get myself used to the change in gears, lowering and lifting the blades and the most important skill, applying the break, I directed the tractor to the tall grass, shouting, "you can kiss your roots goodbye.

I drove for several hours, stopping only to drink some water and for lunch at noon. I returned to finish the job cutting the two acres of our backyard. I loved the smell of the cut grass and the tractor's movement and the feeling of accomplishment. I finished the backyard area and the front of the ranch, again visible in all its orange and brown ugliness. I turned off the tractor, climbing down; my muscles were starting to feel sore; I walked in and told my ex, "It's all done." My ex was still seated on the couch, surrounded by books studying for an upcoming exam.

I couldn't have imagined that my ex would see my defiance and unwillingness to give up on a task as unfeminine and unat-tractive. My "wildness," as he called it, was "unfit to a woman of class." I had embarrassed him that day, hurting his pride.

I should have declined the challenge of driving the tractor, remaining "demure and delicate." which was of course the complete opposite of me.

His words to me, "You will see," still echoed in my mind as I lay in bed, surrounded by the oppressive silence of the ranch.

# Chapter 16

## *Scorpion's March*

The next day, my ex and I took a long walk; we stepped on the ground that the tall grass had hidden. The sheared vegetation was now lying everywhere like a humongous shag carpet.

The tractor had cut down the reeds, leaving behind the remnants that we, in our complete ignorance of ground maintenance, had never considered needing to be collected and disposed of somehow. The grass/tractor experience showed how little we know about each other and country living.

That morning we walked and talked about possible ways for the vegetation to "disappear," such as rabbits and deer feasting on the cut grass until nothing was left. We pondered if we would create a habitat for the rabbit and the deer, who would live in our backyard, waiting for the grass to grow again. We had as much knowledge of animal husbandry as we had of plant management.

The ground was humid from the early morning dew, and dirt and mud soon formed under our feet.

Queenie ran around rapidly changing colors as her grey fur got caked with wet soil.

She ran by us, looking like she was wearing brown boots.

My ex sighed as he jumped from one semi-dry spot to another, trying to spare his shoes and holding his pants legs up, muttering under his breath, "Lodo por todas las partes, caramba"! He was correct; there was mud everywhere.

We turned around and returned to the ranch, arriving with our knee-high mud boots. Queenie followed us, apparently ecstatic with the mud treatment on her skin. The bloom was rapidly falling from the roses of living in the countryside.

My ex removed his shoes at the door and entered the house; he walked to the kitchen and the garage, opening the garage door for me as I carried my now brown dog to the sink next to the washer and dryer. I turned on the water, mixing hot and cold until it reached the perfect temperature for Queenie the Queen.

A pile of soft towels, shampoo, conditioners, and toys lined up on the garage shelves. I carefully placed cotton balls for her ears as I cheerfully spoke to her trying to distract her from the bath, which temporarily turned Queenie into the Tasmanian devil from the Looney Tunes. Queenie required two lather and rinse cycles to return her original color. I gave her some cheese as a peace offering as she shivered, bundled up in a towel in my lap as we sat in the warm kitchen.

My ex emerged from his shower and handed me his muddy pants and socks. Queenie was now on the ground, rolling on the shag carpet, zooming with her head down and her rump up in the air drying off her muzzle and mustache. I watched her amusing antics for a minute. I then took off my pants and socks, wearing my shirt and undies. Collecting all the items for the wash, I opened the kitchen door stepping on the stairs that led to the garage and the washer and dryer.

I could hear a clicking sound like fingernails hitting a hard surface. I felt the wall looking for the light switch; the weather had turned from chilly gray to torrential rain darkening the skies and the garage. The clicking sounds continued; I finally found the light switch, the light flooded the open garage, and the source of the clicking sounds became visible.

I let go of the clothes and I jumped back into the kitchen, leaving the door with only enough space for one of my eyes to see.

I looked at the army of black scorpions hitting the cement floor, the claws and hard shells making the clicking sound I had heard.

I was speechless I looked through my brain for a reasonable explanation for what I was seeing.

I closed the door and took a sip of water, I opened the door again, and the scorpions were still there, clicking their way into the back of my garage. They looked much bigger than the scorpions I had seen in the *National Geographic* magazines.

I looked back at my ex, who sat at the kitchen table sipping tea and leisurely flipping the newspaper pages.

I looked back to the garage, hoping again that the scorpions were only the product of my overactive imagination.

I stared at the creatures that continued to crawl in my garage, making a sickening clicking sound.

My ex had put down his tea and was observing me as he tapped his foot, waiting for an explanation.

I slammed the door behind me and asked my ex to "please, be calm." Talking to myself and my ex at the same time.

"Que esta passando?" he shouted. "What is going on?"

I took a deep breath; "Well," I said as calmly as I could, "it seems that we have a biblical plague in the garage."

My ex's one eyebrow assumed its position for curiosity and annoyance. My ex got up, approached me, removed my hand from the door handle, and opened the door, looking in the garage for one second before slamming the door closed.

"See, I yelled we have big black scorpions in the garage"!

My ex joined me in the hysterics by waving his hands around before putting on oven mitts and grabbing a frying pan.

He puffed up his chest, opened the garage door, and let out high pitch yell as he hurled the frying pan onto the ten or more critters before slamming the door shut.

We were silent, listening for any clicking sound, hoping my ex's actions had sent the critters away.

Once we stopped the heavy breathing, we heard their claws marching in the garage.

For the third time since arriving in America, we had to dial 911.

After looking out in the garage twice more for a visual confirmation that the scorpions were still there, I dialed 911; dispatch got our address. Then the conversation became confusing for all parties involved.

The female dispatcher asked in a monotone voice, "Are they your scorpions?" That question sounded absurd to me; we kill scorpions in Brazil; only a degenerate would keep scorpions in their home!

At that moment, I realized I had the perfect opportunity to use the elegant words "Pardon me?" I asked her to "pardon me," loving the sound of it, my ADD brain focusing away as it always did in moments of curiosity or danger.

My ex's crazy gesticulations and his mouthing "What is going on now" brought me back to the mortal danger we seemed to have found ourselves, as an army of scorpions surrounded us.

Dispatch repeated the question, "Are they yours? Did they escape the terrarium?"

I thought she was asking if we were experiencing "terror." Finally, I thought, we are getting somewhere here.

"Yes," I answered, "big terror here, come fast, " and I hung up the phone, unaware I had to stay on the line until the police arrived.

My ex walked to the bay window to look for the police.

They arrived a few minutes later, and so did an ambulance and a fire truck. They all jumped out of their respective vehicles and quickly approached the opened door. We saw two burly police officers and three equally large firefighters wearing yellow jackets and helmets; one was carrying a flashlight. Another fireman stood there casually, holding an axe. I remember the firefighter holding an axe when he had come to our aid in Cincinnati when we thought we had giant rats at our sliding door that turned out to be something called Opposums. This time was different, I thought to myself; we have venomous creeping creatures, hundreds of them. We may end up on the nightly news, I thought to myself. That was when I realized I was wearing my flannel shirt; my pants had remained in the garage, tossed with the rest of the dirty clothes. I yelled, "Sorry," and ran to my bedroom to find pants, leaving my ex with our saviors in the living room, momentarily distracted by my fast exit.

I slipped into a pair of pants and ran back to the living room, holding Queenie in my arms as she growled at the strangers in our home.

My ex pointed to the garage and said, "Scorpions, there." He still had on the oven mittens he had put on before throwing the frying pan on the critters. The police and the firefighters moved quickly towards the garage door; they opened the door stepping into the garage, they were fearless.

One second later, one of the firefighters walked back in, unharmed; he was smiling, and in his gloved hand, he carried two black scorpions. "These are not scorpions," he said. "These are craw daddies, crayfish, you know?" he asked us.

We were still trying to process what he was saying; we recognized the word "daddy. Was he saying that these were the scorpions' fathers? My ex pointed to the squirming critters and said, "This scorpion's daddy"?

I pulled my ex's arm to get his attention. "So we may have craw moms and craw babies around? I was ready to move out. I wanted to sleep in a motel with lots of asphalt around, so we could have a good night's sleep without fearing that the whole 'cray' family was trying to break in."

Before the Google and smartphone era, trying to explain the difference between a scorpion and a crayfish to English-challenged people was somewhat tricky, coupled with the fact that we were not well-versed in identifying or eating shellfish, which are not found on a Kosher menu.

We followed the firefighter to the garage, where he used a broom to sweep all the craw mommies and daddies into a bucket.

He patiently pointed to the area where a little creek crossed the property; he told us that these critters lived in rivers and streams, and despite their fearsome appearance, they were harmless and, "They taste good in a seafood boil"! He told us that the heavy rain caused them to leave the creek bed as the water level rose. "It looks like the whole area around the creek has recently been cut down," he continued, they must have gotten disoriented, and the whole bunch ended up in your garage!

The rain had finally stopped, and all of Ohio's bravest and finest in the ranch left, returning to help Ohioans with real emergencies.

My ex and I walked into the empty garage hitting the automatic door button and bringing down the heavy door. We agreed that we should never again open the garage door "just in case." We will continue to park in the gravel driveway, rain or shine, making it possible for a quick escape if necessary.

I went in for a shower, finally dressed in clean clothes; my stomach was growling, and I quickly made my way to the kitchen, where I prepared sandwiches that we ate huddled together on the sofa.

We talked for a long time, discussing the harrowing event we had just experienced. We munched on chips and finished the meal with ice cream straight from the container. By the time we were done eating, we were both exhausted.

We took Queenie for a walk holding our flashlights and wearing galoshes as we made our way to the end of the driveway, jumpy at any sound coming from the woods around us.

The air had turned bitterly cold as we walked back to the ranch when we saw the first snowflakes coming down. I became giddy with delight at the site of my first snow. We stood there in the dark, mouths open as we tasted the snow.

After stomping our feet at the door, we settled back on the sofa by the bay window, bundled up in blankets and watching the snow coming down.

The glistening white blanket muffled all sounds but the occasional noise of a tree branch breaking off and falling silently in the snow. My ex and Queenie had drifted off to sleep. I rested my head on my ex's shoulder; maybe, I thought, perhaps this ranch was not a bad idea after all. The snow still falling had silenced my gut feelings, and I finally fell into a dreamless sleep.

# Chapter 17

## *The Goblin*

Monday morning started early with the sounds of the plow guy driving his pick-up truck fitted with a plow attached to the truck chassis that quickly cleared our long gravel driveway and into a path to where we would park our Pontiac Grand Prix.

He had been so kind as to shovel a track from the parking area to our door. I jumped out of bed and brewed some strong coffee; I went out to meet the plow guy holding a cup of steaming coffee for him. He finished shoveling the area that led to the ranch entrance and greeted me with a friendly "Moornin"! He accepted the hot coffee drinking it in big gulps.

I wondered how he could swallow the liquid with steam billowing from the cup. We stood there for a minute, and he finished his coffee, handing me his cup and the invoice for clearing the snow.

The name of his company was "Graham's Landscape"; he thanked him for his coffee and accepted the cash I handed him.

"Thank you…Gra-ham," I said, careful to pronounce his name with an audible "H."

"You're welcome," he responded, "but my name is Graaam,

not Gra-ham." I apologized, wondering why using an "H" in his name and then not using it when pronouncing the name.

I apologized for mispronouncing his name, and he gave me a friendly smile and told me "not to worry." I smiled back, knowing that I wouldn't worry at all but was appreciative of this apparent concern for my emotions.

Graaam left, and I stood at the door for a few minutes, enjoying the view of the property covered in fluffy snow. The plow had created small hills of snow, not precisely the Swiss Alps mountains of my childhood's favorite movie, *The Sound of Music*, but it was good enough to walk up to the top and then roll down, laying on the fresh snow and making snow angels.

That was my plan after my ex left for school, leaving Queenie and me to frolic on the snow of my dreams.

I walked back in and went to the kitchen to wash the cups and prepare my ex a hearty breakfast.

My ex was up an hour later; he walked into the kitchen, already dressed for his day. He sat at the table and ate his breakfast while reading the newspaper. He finished his coffee and returned to our bedroom to wear his snow outfit.

He had emerged wearing a puffy winter jacket over several layers of clothing, heavy snow boots, and a hat with lapels covering his ears that, while unfastened, gave him the appearance of a bloodhound. He pronounced he was ready to brave the snow and leave for the University. He walked to the car carrying his books; Neil Armstrong's famous saying came to me as I watched him walk towards the car, "That's one small step for man, one giant leap for mankind who has never walked on snow."

He drove off slowly, aware of his inexperience in driving on snow. My ex's careful and deliberate disposition would get on my nerves sometimes, as I am sure my impulsive or rather "proactive" temperament would get on his nerves.

Still, in this instance, I was grateful for how slowly he drove down our driveway, and I knew he would take his time driving the 45 minutes it took to get to the University.

I finished my chores, eager to leave for the outdoors where * could breathe the fresh cold air.

The initial feeling of the somber dampness of the ranch continued unabated despite my many efforts to brighten up the home.

I would draw out the curtains, hoping the light coming in through the window would cut away through the oppressiveness of the dark paneled walls and the shag carpet that muffled our steps in the living room and bedrooms.

The paintings leftover from our art dealing days were hanging on the walls. The carefully arranged knick-knacks and accent lamps only contrasted with the stubborn sadness that clung everywhere inside the ranch.

Growing up in Brazil, I would listen to the folklore of haunted houses, ghosts, and the mysterious creatures that lived deep in the Amazon forests.

"The headless mule" haunted ranchers by setting fire to everything in its path by blowing fire through its nose. Brazilians never doubted or discussed the mule's headless condition and ability to blow fire from his nostrils.

The stories of the pink dolphins swimming in the Amazon rivers that would sing and entice the local women in the village would emerge from the river, shapeshifting into handsome men. The pink dolphin, called "Boto," would lure women into romance and, after impregnating them, would disappear into the river's dark waters, never to be seen again. That was the agreed-upon explanation for the unexpected pregnancies in the Amazon villages.

If something went missing in a Brazilian home, "The Saci Perere" was the culprit, a one-legged creature naked but for a red cap he wore on his head and a pipe that he smoked while causing mischief in people's lives.

The Saci was said to travel inside a dust devil (a small-scale dust hurricane, not the vacuum cleaner), and he could be captured and held in a glass bottle, where he would remain until granting his captor a wish. That was risky because once you liberated the Saci from the bottle, you would incur its wrath, and mischief could turn malicious.

The Saci would return, riding the headless mule, gushing fire through its incomprehensible nostrils. You could befriend Saci by giving him Brazilian Tequila "Cachaca" or tobacco for his pipe.

Tales of Jewish mysticism make several references to the Divine and the supernatural. Any other argument could not explain my parents' escape from certain death in the concentration camps other than Divine and supernatural forces.

Even in the cheery and tropical Sun in Brazil their memory of the six million Jews who perished in the extermination camps, including their family members, clung to my parents' consciousness, imbuing it with prolonged bouts of survivor's guilt. As I walked through the drab ranch's rooms I would recall the former owners' cruelty towards their aging dog, shooting it and leaving it in the garage to die, alone and scared, waiting to be found by us, the unsuspecting new owners of the property.

Their abhorrent act suggested souls filled with cruelty and depravity; their darkness had sipped through each fabric, brick, and wood grain of the ranch, causing its dampening of all light and joy.

The weird vibe of the home triggered my gut feeling that something was very wrong with the place, from the moment I stepped into the property.

I took Queenie out for a long walk in the snow, hoping to lose the ranch sadness while walking in the fresh snow and breathing the clean air. I must have walked for several miles on the 33 Acres of the property. The tall trees stood naked but for the accumulated snow in their branches.

I returned to the ranch; Queenie and I stood soaked from the snow melting off our shoes and clothes. I towel driedthe shivering Queenie and gave her an early dinner; she scoffed the meal, and in seconds, she was snoring on the sofa.

I felt better after the long walk; and the steamy shower. I prepared dinner, expecting my ex to return to the ranch any minute.

He walked in a half-hour later carrying a pile of clothes; he had stripped each layer of clothing as he sweated in the heated classrooms, returning home wearing only a turtleneck shirt under the puffy jacket. We ate dinner and talked about our days; we retired to our bedroom early that night. We were exhausted by our new experiences and emotions regarding adapting to a new environment and culture.

I fell asleep with the ranch sorrow covering me as an extra blanket. I woke up in a panic, startled and unable to move. Cold sweat was pouring down my face as I, my eyes adjusted to the darkness, I could hear the heavy breathing and smelled the fetid breath of the winged Goblin sitting on my chest, staring at me with green eyes and a wide, contorted smile that revealed two rows of sharp teeth. The creature had scaly and bumpy skin, the broad wings outstretched, revealing a taut bat-like structure with spikes protruding from each wingtip.

I tried to move or call out to my ex, but I was paralyzed.

I had no voice or the ability to move. I lay there feeling the creature's weight pressing my chest. The Goblin's long, spiked nails were close to my face, the fingers with membrane encircling each section, the muscles in its scaly arms throbbing, now visible by the moonlight coming through the window.

The creature's fetid breath made it hard for me to breathe. I remembered my father who had taught me a prayer to be said in times of danger. I closed my eyes and murmured the powerful Hebrew prayer where we proclaimed and assert that the Lord is all-powerful and the Lord is one. I repeated the prayer until I could feel the weight of the creature lift from my chest, letting me finally get a full deep breath.

The creature was gone. The faint putrid smell emanating from its open mouth dissipated slowly.

I had recovered my ability to move, I jumped off the bed, and opened the window, thrusting my sweaty face into the cold night.

I looked around the room, scared out of my mind by the experience. My ex slept soundly, unaware of the horrific creature that had landed on my chest seconds before.

I wanted to wake him up and tell him about the ordeal. I stood there weighing the pros and cons of waking my ex up with a story he would most likely dismiss while asserting that I was superstitious and unreasonable, prone to excessive imagination from a lifetime of exposure to anecdotes that made no sense.

He would have chastised me for waking him up from much-needed sleep to tell him fanciful tales that sounded like the mystical tales of Ghetto European Jews like my parents.

My ex often used that argument after marriage whenever he disagreed with me on religious practices, faith, and fate.

He would pontificate arrogantly calling the source of my parents' limitless faith, superstition. His lack of compassion infuriated me and was the start of the chasm between us, widening slowly and further distancing each other as we painfully realized that we did not belong together.

I felt utterly alone as I joined my ex in bed; I curled up with Queenie in my arms., as I recalled Queenie's low whimpering as she lay by the foot of our bed while the creature sat on my chest, so Quennie had seen it too, too bad she couldn't talk. Queenie licked away my tears and the remaining sweat droplets from my face. She placed her face on my shoulder, and a few seconds later, she was fast asleep. Holding my sweet ball of fur, I relaxed, and shortly after, I fell asleep.

# Chapter 18

## *Duty And The Ties That Bind*

The morning after the Goblin sat on my chest, I was done with the ranch and trying to ignore my gut feeling that would stubbornly emerge as it tried to communicate the wisdom of my brain and my heart.

I lay next to my sleeping ex; Queenie crawled out of my arms to go lay down in her usual place at the foot of the bed.

The Goblin was gone, leaving in its place the terrible memory associated with sleeping in that room with my new husband to whom I should have been able to tell anything good or bad..

I remembered my parents' advice always to balance reason and feelings.

I wished I could talk to my ex about my feelings and my experience the night before. However, I had to consider my ex's disdain for anything not explained by math or science.

My ex would have responded to my apparition tale by retreating emotionally and physically from me. He would then assume the physical posture of an annoyed professor looking at his dimwitted student. Aloof, his silence in haughty disapproval would often cause me to doubt my memory, my intelligence and worth.

I was tired from the frightening experience. I closed my

eyes, and suddenly the memory of the man I was dating before my ex came to me. I could not send those memories back to where they came from that day. I had been seeing my first serious boyfriend for almost a year, and we were starting to get serious when my dad approached me one day, asking me to go on a date he had arranged. I was surprised by the request since my parents seemed relieved to see me finally settling with someone whom I was very fond of, experiencing for the first time the closest emotion to love. The man had been introduced to me by friends of my parents which I assumed they approved.

I hesitated, wanting to tell my dad how much I liked my current boyfriend; however, my dad's pleading eyes and hopeful smile made it impossible for me to say no. Several years later, I sat at a therapist's office, where we poured through the events that followed my father's request that day.

I had learned year's later and too late to save that relationship that a child of Holocaust survivors would often substitute their own needs, interests, and desires for those of their parents to fill the void left in their parents' hearts by the loss of their families and friends at the brutal hands of the Nazis.

My parents' memories of unrelenting fear, torture, and pain remained in an easily accessible place in their minds and bodies. My mother's migraines would materialize when she heard about a friend, family, or even a stranger's tragedy.

I remembered my mother's panicked look as we walked the streets of Frankfurt on a layover to Israel. My mom had stopped in the middle of a busy street in Frankfurt while the passersby chatted to each other in German, stepping aside as she continued to stand there immobile, her eyes unblinking, her chest heaving matching her rapid breathing.

They people in the street that day were unaware they were walking by an empty body as her soul had returned to the barracks in the Majdanek concentration camp. My mother entered the camp as a prisoner at thirteen until liberation when she turned eighteen. My mother walked the fine line between life and death daily in Majdanek.

She dared to jump from her line selected for the gas chambers to the line of those who got to live another day, at risk of being shot each time. My mother stood on that street that day; her eyes fixed forward as tears fell down her cheeks. I called her, approaching where she stood. Suddenly, her mouth opened and she screamed in German, "I am here, I survived."

She started walking towards me and asked me if I was hungry and if we should look for a restaurant. I looked at her, and she smiled back at me; she pinched my cheeks and called me "little bird," her pet name. "Let's go; I am starving!" she exclaimed. We walked side by side; I didn't need to ask what had just happened.

I knew that the startled passerby and I had just witnessed my mother shedding one layer of pain from the several layers that inhabited her body and soul for so long. I grew up believing that my parents' happiness was my siblings' and my responsibility; we were alive as the result of their miraculous survival.

My brother was to be studious and earn a decent living through an honorable trade, and he had to marry a woman who would honor him and the family. My sister and I could study, but marrying and having children were our primary goals. My sister graduated from college with a literature BA, and the race to find a husband was on after graduation.

She was beautiful, and she had her pick among many suitors. She enjoyed getting dolled up and meeting the hopeful men she dated and promptly discarded if the poor guy would earn my parents' disfavor for whatever reason. My sister was dutiful and compliant, discussing her options for potential grooms with my mom.

A groom was finally selected when I turned twelve, and my sister was twenty-four. I liked him because he had given me a very cool plastic watch, instantly earning my affection.

I, on the other hand, was not overtly compliant or dutiful. I kept my indebtedness to my parents' happiness hidden by rebellion and mischief.

I wanted to be free to do what interested me; I loved art and painted and drew on every surface available at home and school from an early age. I loved science, history, and animals. I tended to get distracted at school but passed each grade without much effort. I told my parents that I was going to be an artist. They admired my artistic skills inherited from my father and his side of the family.

My brother had also shown talent in art, and his paintings attracted the attention of a renowned local artist who had offered to tutor his brother for free. My mom nixed the artistic ambitions for both myself and my brother. She told us the story of Vincent Van Gogh and his sad life of madness and poverty that led him to lop off one of his ears.

My mother's talent as a storyteller had us spellbound, horrified and grateful that she had prevented us from meeting the same fate as the extraordinary Dutch artist.

My brother went on to study psychology, and he never painted again. I continued drawing and painting any chance I got.

I worked during the day and attended college at night.

During those years, I was dropped off at youth gatherings at our synagogue to begin my social interactions with possible suitors. When I turned 18, many of my high school classmates had already married, engaged, or were seriously dating.

I would come home after these gatherings, take off my shoes and plop down on my bed, content in my solitude. I would read from an immense pile of books I had brought home from the library while listening to Classical music on the turntable.

I was used to being alone from an early age, and I was not too fond of small talk, seeing the practice as an unwelcome intrusion into my world where my imagination had no bounds. I kept my friend group of like-minded people small, but it was enough for methe last child born to family. My soul had resisted making an appearance in the world, most likely entertained by the mysteries of the universe and whatever else souls do to pass the time. My maturity level lagged behind those of my peers. My parents and older siblings were busy with their day-to-day lives. They were happy to leave me be unless I got into trouble. My small circle of friends would meet outside our buildings after school, daring each other to go into the "haunted house" neighborhood or jump from high places while riding our bikes and rollerblading. As we grew into adolescence, I saw some of my friends holding hands with each other and kissing behind bushes.

I remember when one of my male friends turned to me with amorous eyes, picking up my hand. I felt his sweaty palm; I broke out from his grip and ran back home, feeling nauseous and excited simultaneously.

I spent my teen years into early adulthood running away from serious relationships. I was well into my mid to late twenties when my parents decided that they needed to take the matter of my slow pace regarding romance into their hands. One of my mother's friends introduced her nephew to me.

He was a tall, dark-haired man with handsome features and an easy-going nature. I liked him immediately and found myself relaxing in someone's embrace for the first time. His scent pleased me, and so did his never-too-wet or too-dry kisses. He would laugh at my antics and join me; I had found the warmth of a friend and a lover's excitement in him.

He had been married before and doted on his little daughter during her visits to his home. I adored kids and bonded with the tiny dark-haired little girl with the exact sweet nature as her dad.

My parents witnessed the change in me; the usually opinionated tomboy who longed for solitude would now watch by the window for the arrival of her beloved. The relationship continued to my parents' surprise.

I would talk to my mom about my feelings for my dark-haired boyfriend. To my surprise and confusion, my mother advised me to go slow; the fact that he was a divorcee weighed heavily on their conservative mind.

Unbeknownst to me, a campaign to find me a more desirable suitor had begun. My father reached out to the senior rabbi at our congregation. He asked to introduce me and my future husband, the synagogue's junior clergyman. My parents had seen my ex and learned he was single during the services. They dreamed of the honor bestowed on them for having one of their children marry a religious man.

One day, I was approached or somewhat "ambushed" by my parents; they both stood in my room looking at me for a second before they asked that I see the young clergyman "just once." I initially turned them down, protesting the intrusion into my current relationship.

The campaign continued, and it reached its peak when my boyfriend, accompanied by his parents, surprised me at my home with an engagement bracelet and a lovely proposal. My mother asked them to sit comfortably in our living room while she spoke to me for a moment in private.

I walked to my bedroom, thinking about why my mother wanted to speak to me alone when I was going to be engaged, realizing their dream of seeing me at the altar.

My mom closed her door behind her; she looked like she was trying to compose her thoughts, and she delivered, in a grave tone, her argument against me accepting my boyfriend's proposal that night.

I listened quietly as my mother urged me not to accept the marriage proposal until I had a chance to meet my parents' choice of suitor, the young clergyman who had called me inviting me on a date just two days prior. I had politely refused his invitation. Somehow my parents became aware that I had rebuked the clergyman's invitation.

My mother warned me that accepting a marriage proposal would create a pact that would bind us to each other forever. She continued in her serious tone that if I broke that sacred promise to unite myself to that person, the dark shadow of judgment would fall upon me, nullifying any attempt I would make to create a happy union with another man.

"A promise given on earth," she continued, "reverberates in heaven, 'as above, so below.'" I listened quietly to my mother's words of warning. I thought about the wordless whispers we uttered as we embraced each other. Words seemed unnecessary as we enjoyed each other in true kinship. Could it be that the connection we shared was being overlooked in heaven?

"How about you and Dad?" I asked. "You remained bound to each other even after Dad's family urged him not to marry you and to look for a woman who did not bore the scars of the Holocaust."

My mother sighed and answered, "Your dad and I went through tough times, and I don't wish on you the difficulties we overcame at the beginning of our marriage. They shared their mutual trauma and extreme poverty as they started their lives together in Israel after being liberated from the concentration camps in Cyprus.

The island of Cyprus housed the Holocaust refugees who had attempted to reach Israel in their ramshackle ships and were rerouted to the island by the British who ruled Israel then.

The island was where my parents' relationship grew and blossomed, and despite the difficult circumstances at that time, they persevered, loving and supporting each other which would go on throughout their lives. I thought about my boyfriend and his parents sitting in the living room with my father in an uncomfortable silence, wondering what was taking so long.

I stood up and told my mom that I was returning to the living room and didn't know what to do.

My mother followed me closely, and before I crossed the threshold to the living room, she held me by my arm and said, "Please, do it for us."

That request may sound absurd to anyone but the children of Holocaust survivors. My parents' happiness depended on my actions and choices. How could I bring more suffering to my parents, who had suffered so much?

I entered the room, avoiding my boyfriend's eyes. I sat next to him, but I had already departed from our union; I felt like a cold second skin enveloped me—the coldness rejecting my boyfriend's tender touch. My soul traveled at light speed, distancing myself from him.

I asked him for some time to think about his proposal. His stunned and pained expression almost brought me back; my parents sat near me, my father embracing my mother.

For a moment, I questioned the whole situation, trying to elicit again the feelings of love and connection I had felt for the first time in a relationship. My parents' suffering and loss in the camps were never far from my mind. Their memories and pain weaved into the fabric of my being.

I could not release myself from the ties that bound my parents' happiness. I would bring them the honor by marrying a religious man, a junior clergyman in the biggest congregation in São Paulo would give them a reason for their miraculous survival.

My boyfriend slipped the box with the bracelet back into his pocket. He helped his mother get up from the sofa, and his father supported his wife as they walked away from my life forever.

My mother hugged me and went to the kitchen to prepare tea for herself and my father. The living room felt empty and hollow, which was the feeling I felt inside my broken heart.

# Chapter 19

## *The Clergyman*

The morning light peeked through the trees and into our bedroom, a sign that it was now mid-morning. I was still in bed, immersed in the memories of my life until that point.

My ex, still asleep, his chest rising and falling rhythmic undisturbed by my thoughts. I looked at his handsome face, blissful in his ignorance of the turmoil next to him.

My ex never knew of the events before I met with him for the first time. We met at a popular restaurant in São Paulo on our first date. I noticed my ex's hovering eye as he directed his attention from our conversation to the women entering and exiting the restaurant with their companions.

I was incredulous at his bold behavior which to me suggested that he would have difficulties with fidelity and monogamy.

We finished our meal, and he drove me home; he planted a quick kiss on my lips and asked me to another date on the coming weekend. I told him, "Sure," and walked into my apartment without looking back.

My mom awaited my return from my first date with my

future ex. We sat in the living room and told my mom of my ex's troublesome behavior at the restaurant. I used the word "philanderer"; I told her how unsettling I felt his behavior to be, especially for a clergyman.

My mother quickly dismissed my observation, declaring that what I was suggesting was "impossible" due to my ex's clergyman status in the most respected Synagogue in our town. She accused me of "making up an excuse to turn down" my ex due to being stubborn and selfish, thinking only about myself my ill-fated relationship with my "divorced"boyfriend who before the clergyman's appearance had been accepted by my parents as suitable "despite being divorced" At that time I was considered "old" in terms of finding the choice matches in my community. My mother urged me to give my ex another chance, "for us," she repeated the request that I had no way of turning down.

I told myself that my mind was playing tricks on me, and I silenced my instincts again. I gave him a chance, and at the end of each date for an entire year, I would enumerate each desirable qualities I found in my ex, no matter how small or imagined.

I turned deaf to my heart longings and the nagging voice of my instincts and blind to my ex's flirtatious behavior. I would focus on my parents' beaming smiles as they proudly walked with me to the congregation's reserved seats, all eyes on the future wife of the young clergyman. Years later, I thought about my ex with sympathy and regret.

He had undoubtedly deserved better than to be loved by what he did instead of by who he was. I had learned to compliment him on all his actions and always to be agreeable.

I met the ex's parents; he looked like his mom, from whom he inherited liquid green eyes, a small nose, and full, fleshy lips. His father was a pleasant but anxious man perpetually harassed by his wife, due to his Tourettes involuntary movements and loud cough. My ex and his older sister were allowed to tease their good natured father. The tale of their union was told to me by my ex, who said that his mother was one of the most desirable

Bachelorette in town due to her beauty and with. My ex's father her pursued her relentlessly ignoring her rejection until he"wore her down" and she finally agreed to marry him. To me the story was more sad than amusing.

I remember seeing the hurt in his father's eyes, who would take the teasing, as if fulfilling his part in the reluctant union with his utterly disinclined bride my ex's mother who had agreed to marry him despite her belief that she had married beneath her. My ex's mother was not enthusiastic about his choosing me as a wife either. I could sense her disapproval coming from every insincere smile and an insults disguised as a jokes.

I always wondered why he chose me, going against his mother's open disdain for his choice. I thought about the impact on my ex's psyche from seeing his father belittled in a marriage that seemed to lack genuine warmth and attraction to one another.

Perhaps that was why my ex could accept the shallowness of our union as long as I did my part which was to look at him as the reason the sun rose each morning and agreeing with every word uttered by him and full filing all his whims and desires without questioning, ever.

The scriptures talk about the sacredness of the union of two souls in marriage. The instructions in the sacred texts are clear about the alliance between two souls that should be free of distractions or subterfuge. Disingenuous emotions will hinder the harmonic exchange of energy between a couple. The goal is to embark on a relationship of equals, face to face, as their bodies and souls bond based on physical attraction and the recognition of their soulmate.

These unions are impervious to the many challenges experienced throughout their lives. They face difficulties together, and each supports the other in a united front which strengthens their marriage as they face each other when needing to gather strength and walk side by side as they look in the same direction into their future.

. In the absence of real kinship and physical attraction I went on to make one of the most importants life decisions based on duty and and indecision regarding my right to create a life based on my needs, interests, and goals. It was easier to relent and do what was expected of me.

The self-betrayal came to me in a dream the night before my wedding. I dreamt that my parents abandoned me, thrown out of our house, and the door shut in my face. I found myself walking inside a hotel, looking for shelter.

I used the elevator to take me to different floors, and each stood occupied by people I knew from high school and college. They were all settled, but there was no room for me. I stopped at the last floor and faced a little girl who reminded me of myself. She was visibly upset, holding an empty jewelry box; she accused me of having stolen the most precious jewels she had. I looked at the little girl, her face stained by tears.

I apologized to her and said, "I am the one who took them from you." She stopped crying and responded, "Thank you for telling me the truth." I looked up, and this time, I found myself looking at my reflection in a large mirror hanging on the wall. I woke up with a startle from my dream; I looked around the hotel suite we had booked for the marriage ceremony.

I knocked at the door to the adjoining room where my parents spent the night. My mom opened the door, and I saw my father sitting in a chair as he listened to my sister's newest crisis. My mother hugged me and asked if I had had breakfast.

I shook my head and waited for an explanation or a chance to tell my parents about my dream.

My sister acknowledged my presence by glancing in my direction before asking for my parents' advice and intervention in her problem with her oldest daughter. My mother sat by my father's side and joined in the conversation.

I returned to my room and closed the door behind me. A knock at my door brought me one of the servers who wheeled into my room the complimentary "Marriage day breakfast," complete with coffee, eggs, and champagne. I was tempted to try a glass of the bubbly drink but decided against it as I had no tolerance for alcohol and would most likely fall asleep missing my marriage ceremony.For a moment that seemed like a viable plan for getting out of the wedding, but what would I do next? I would have caused my parents shame and embarrassment and the cost of the wedding.

A few minutes later, the hairdresser and the makeup artist showed up. As they set up their workstation, my parents emerged from the adjoining room with my sister, now accompanied by her twelve-year-old daughter. The latter was a constant annoyance to my sister, who often turned to my parents and me to referee their latest conflict.

My niece was the product of my sister's first failed marriage, who, through no fault of her own, was a constant reminder to my sister of her disastrous first marriage that lasted seven months before it broke down. My sister returned to my parents' home pregnant with my niece. I felt like I was back in my dream; my mother and sister occupied with their hair and makeup, talking about hairstyles with the hairdresser, and my father was watching TV with my niece.

It felt like I was back in my dream, "outside looking in."

The next few hours passed by quickly, and the hair and makeup stylist finished getting us ready and left; the caterer and multiple staff from the hotel would come in and out as they checked the final details of the ceremony and the dinner served afterward.

The last check-in came from the hired orchestra band leader, who got the music requests and left to set up in the hotel's events hall.

I was ready at six past ten, fashionably late. I walked the aisle holding my proud father's arm. My ex stood under the marriage canopy, looking handsome in a beautiful dark suit.

My future ex-mother-in-law wore a long black dress, gloves up to her elbows, a-la Morticia Adams, and bright red lipstick.

My future ex-sister-in-law stood by her parents, also wearing black, making a noticeable contrast to my mother and my siblings' light color scheme in their outfits.

The night ended with lots of toasts and good wishes to the newlyweds. It was over, I thought to myself, or rather this is the beginning. I am a married woman; I am Mrs so and so. As it had always been, I spent a good deal of time entertained by my thoughts as my ex slept beside me.

I looked at the clock on my side table; it was eleven fifteen, way past our usual wake-up time. I sat on the bed, ready to get up and take Queenie out to do her business. I was still unsure how I would tell my ex of the apparition from the night before and tell him that I couldn't possibly spend one more night on the ranch.

My ex stirred in his sleep, letting out a big yawn.

He opened his eyes and looked at me; his green eyes closely matched the color of the ghoul from the previous night, complete with redness surrounding his pupils.

I smiled at him, opening my mouth to greet him lovingly. Instead, a flurry of words came out in one breath; "I can't stay here anymore; I hate this ranch; you are not going to believe what happened to me last night; I saw a Goblin sitting on my chest; it was so scary, I couldn't move, I want to get out of here!!"

My ex's left eyebrow went up, reaching the top of his forehead, so high that I became concerned that his eyebrow would get stuck there permanently.

"Que estas hablando?" What are you saying? he asked; the annoyance on his face sent me crawling back to my safe place in the deepest recondite of my body.

I thought I had gone too far to stop now; I couldn't tell him "just kidding" or "April's fool" as it was December.

On rare occasions, my ex seemed to appreciate my brand of comic relief. However, that morning in Cincinnati, he must have sensed that I wasn't joking and probably thought that he had now enough evidence to send me away to an extended stay in a facility with well-padded rooms.

I avoided his quizzical look; I got up, entered the bathroom, and closed the door. I looked in the mirror; my hair stood where I had twirled it, a nervous habit that had me looking like I had allowed a couple of birds to nest on my head.

I took a shower, emerging from it invigorated and ready to provide my ex with breakfast and an explanation for my outburst.

My ex was in the kitchen tinkering with the coffee maker and grumbling to himself in Spanish. I told him that I would take over making us breakfast.

My ex stepped away and, from a safe distance, asked, "Are you feeling better?" His look reaffirmed my suspicion that he was closer than ever to considering a psychiatric stay for me.

He was a clergyman on the fast track to receiving a Master's degree in Religious Studies. Still, his view on the intangible, unseen, and unexplained was that it was the product of the imagination of a superstitious or unbalancedmind. My ex was readily irritated by my willingness to consider alternative explanations to unexplained circumstances well as my unshakable faith in God, refusing to call it "belief," a word that insinuates doub in my opinion. My ex's anger would bring on long soliloquous regarding superstition and the ignorance of the masses regarding religion which to me was incredibly odd coming from someone who chose to sacedorcy and a religion as a profession.

I sat at the kitchen table holding my cup of coffee as I waited for my ex to eat a few bites of his croissant, timing our conversation to commence after he had consumed enough carbs to settle his nerves. After a minute or so, I cleared my throat; it felt a bit scratchy; I took another sip of my coffee and told my ex what had happened during the night as he slept.

My ex listened to me as he continued to chew his food. He drank his coffee as I waited for his response.

He was silent as he retrieved a handkerchief from his sweater pocket to blow his nose. I noticed his face was flushed, and his eyes were tearing as he prepared himself for an incoming sneeze.

Suddenly my ex stood up and announced in a shaky voice, "I don't feel too well." He ran out of the kitchen; I followed him, wondering if he was trying to avoid an argument which would have been unlike him. My ex welcomed any chance he had to argue in favor or against any topics. That day, he went into the restroom, and soon, I could hear his vomiting sounds.

I was uncertain if perhaps my story had inexplicably made him ill. I thought to myself, "Wow, how ironic, I am the one who had a ghoul sit on my chest, and he is the one who vomits."

I heard the water running in the sink, and my ex emerged from the bathroom; his face had a greenish tinge; he took a few steps moaning, and dropped his body on the bed.

"I think I may be dying," he said in a weak voice. His statement sent me into action; I was determined to save him.

I handed him a glass of water and a thermometer. His face had changed from pale green to red. He lay on his pillow with his arms crossed, holding the thermometer under his arm. He kept his eyes closed.

I had never seen my ex sick or as vulnerable as he looked at that moment. After a minute, he handed me the thermometer; I looked at it, freezing in place once I saw his temperature. I looked at it again, holding it closer to my eyes. I could not believe what I saw; the temperature was 102 degrees, which meant my ex was melting in front of my eyes as the highest temperature I had ever heard in my life was my mother's 41 degree fever during a illness she had in Brazil.

My ex saw my panicked look and reminded me that I was looking at a temperature measured in Fahrenheit and not Celsius like in Brazil.

I breathed a sigh of relief; I was dizzy from holding my breath and felt nauseous. I went looking for Tylenol and brought it back to him. I placed a tall glass of orange juice on his side table and left again to make him some tea.

I heard my ex sneeze again, and seconds later, he whimpered.

Ok, I thought to myself, the man has a bad cold from the looks of it. At least he is not in the process of melting, I imagined having to collect my liquified ex into some sort of container, careful to not spill lest Imloose one of his limbs or appendage. I sat at the kitchen table laughing at my weird thoughts, I rested my head on my hand as I, waited for the water to boil to make him some tea. I was feeling tired and dizzy as well as nauseous. I chalked up my symptoms related to the frightening figure that sat on my chest during the night and from almost becoming a widow.

I noticed however that I had started dropping diagonally until my head rested on the table. I felt the cooling surface on my face. I tried to prop myself up, but my arm would start sliding, and soon I had my face resting on the table again. How odd, I thought, when I suddenly let out a big sneeze, scaring myself and barely avoiding a traumatic brain injury by missing the table top by a few inches. I stood up, and a wave of nausea came upon me.

I sneezed twice on my way to retrieve the thermometer from my ex. By the time I had it under my arm, I knew that my ex and I had both acquired some mysterious illness.

I checked my temperature, which measured one degree lower than my ex. After walking Queenie for a few minutes, I made tea and carried it to our room.

My ex had bundled himself with an extra blanket and was sleeping, his breathing sounding congested. I lay next to him, suddenly noticing that every joint in my body hurt. I downed two Tylenol tablets, and soon, I was also asleep.

We both woke up at the same time as the night was falling.

My ex was now coughing and hacking while I joined in with several sneezes in a row. There was no question in our minds that we were both suffering from the worse cold-like illness ever.

My ex proclaimed that he was sicker and older than me and needed me to care for him. I replied that I felt like my head was about to fall off, and he was only two years older than me.

We were too sick to continue arguing, so we remained in bed, getting up to retrieve another box of kleenex, tea, and orange juice and to let Queenie out.

We spent the night sweating and rolling around in the sheets, looking for a cool and dry spot. I joined my ex in the coughing and hacking symphony, and we felt worse the next day.

We got dressed and looked in the yellow pages for the nearest hospital. My ex drove us; bless his heart, craning his neck close to the windshield to see the road through his teary eyes filled with congestion. We walked into the brightly lit emergency room and joined a room full of people who were also coughing, sneezing, and moaning.

A doctor saw us both at the same time. The doctor wore a mask as if he was getting ready for surgery. Oh lord, I thought to myself, are we so sick that we may need surgery? What kind of surgery?, I wondered in my febrile state; an amusing thought started to percolate as I thought of nose removal surgery as a recommended treatment to stop sneezing. I laughed, which in turn, caused me a prolonged coughing fit. The kind doctor had finished our exams; he informed us that we had "The Flu."

He told us that half the country was suffering from this ailment that would reappear yearly in people's bodies during the Winter. The Flu vaccine didn't exist then, and even if it did, it wouldn't have helped our Flu was "in full bloom" in our bodies.

We were sent home with Codeine cough syrup and told to rest and keep ourselves hydrated. My ex drove us to the pharmacy to pick up the cough syrup and an ample supply of kleenex and juice. We made it home, and I took Queenie to do her business.

I returned to see my sweating ex carrying our mattress to the living room. My ex stripped the sweaty sheets, and we worked together, placing fresh linen on the mattress on the living room floor.

We had taken the cough syrup, and soon, we both felt the first narcotic effects of the Codeine that eased the constant cough.

I rested my head on his outstretched arm. I kissed him on the cheek, and he hugged me. There was no need to discuss the Goblin; my ex had acknowledged the distressing experience by moving the heavy mattress to a Goblin-free area.

# Chapter 20

## *The Exit Flu*

My ex and I had our first American experience that was utterly horrible. I had never been so sick, and neither did my ex.

We had both experienced a cold, even a bad one; the Flu was in a particular category of misery delivery.

I had my share of childhood illnesses, with chicken pox and mumps being the worst until I had the Flu. Interestingly, we don't have the Flu in Brazil, despite living with "creative" water and sewer systems and drinking water from the faucet for our entire lives.

My parents had an apartment in the beach town of Guaruja, a beautiful vacation spot 90 minutes from São Paulo. The condo was technically beachfront since you could see a sliver of the beach between the buildings that lined up the actual waterfront.

The most important feature of the apartment was its location, several streets away from the open sewer that ran through the whole city, depositing the detritus straight into the ocean.

The presence of the open sewers that let their contents into the open ocean water was never a concern to the thousands of beachgoers that would spend their days lying in the sun, eating the delicious foods sold by beach vendors.

For those old enough to drink, the "caipirinha" was free-flowing; the lemon, sugar, cachaca – a 90-proof alcohol – and crushed ice were served in little shot glasses.

Food is everywhere: tiny fried fish and unidentified meat in skewers sold as chicken or meat, cassava biscuits, salty and delicious. Fresh coconut and succulent slices of pinnacle waited to be purchased, laying on huge slabs of ice.

To the children's delight, vendors peddled beach balls, colorful pinwheels, balloons, straw hats, and jute mats.

Music is everywhere as spontaneous Samba playing occurs amid the beachgoers who join in with improvised instruments as any hard surface could drum up a "batuque." Some would bring real samba instruments providing the spectators with the irresistible samba beat.

Going to the beach in Brazil is a whole day's endeavor. You go to the beach in the early morning to claim the best spot for the mat, chairs, and beach umbrellas, away from the sewer discharge into the ocean. Social and romantic relationships begin and end between the people strolling around with athletic and toned bodies, sometimes joining a beach volleyball game while dunking themselves in the cool waves to get relief from the sun.

Getting a tan is a serious business in Brazil, where a dark tan is seen as a status symbol of those rich enough to spend their time lying in the sun all day. Achieving the perfect tan requires the beachgoer to alternate swimming in the ocean and laying back down on the jute mat while reapplying the commercial skin bronzer or the homemade concoction of baby oil, Coca Cola, and a few drops of iodine mixture in their whole body.

My ex and I spent weekends on the beach in Guaruja. My ex had only one experience of swimming in the ocean in Brazil.

He had gone in the water, jumping in and swimming away in apparent delight until he was face to face with a floating brown mass that appeared to have been carried by the current from the sewer discharge a few miles away.

I saw him swimming at high speed to the shore and exiting

the water with a combination of high jumps and strides toward the sand. He ran to the apartment, where he took a long shower that required repeated lathering of his whole body with soap and gargling with salt water simultaneously.

That was his last swim in the Atlantic Ocean in the beautiful resort town of Guaruja.

Back in Cincinnati, my ex and I started to feel better two weeks after the first signs of the Flu. Being sick and driving 45 minutes to his University took its toll on my ex. Slowly we started to discuss our shared dissatisfaction with life at the ranch. We agreed that we had been a tad impulsive when we tried to achieve all the American dreams at the same time just months after arriving in this Blessed country.

We were still sleeping on the mattress in the living room, which seemed to work on preventing the return of the Goblin. The spring weather started, and the grass was turning green again, which meant that the growing grass would require lots of mowing.

After hiring the tractor to tame the forest of weeds, we purchased an electric mower since the gas-powered mower seemed dangerous for a cigarette smoker like my ex. We soon discovered that mowing the entire area required several miles of power cords and well-appointed outlets. Fortunately, the snow started soon after the first mow, and nothing grew for several months.

The property went up for sale a few weeks later. Each day that started, we would stare hopefully at the home phone, waiting to hear from the same real estate broker who had sold us the property.

He didn't seem surprised to see us back at his office; he agreed to represent us on the sale of the 33-acre ranch in Loveland, Ohio. We hired a construction and landscaping company and kept the house's interior and exterior pristine. We were both developing good muscle tone from moving the mattress to the

Goblin suite each morning and bringing it back to the living room at night.

The Goblin saga was never again discussed; however, my ex's willingness to move the heavy mattress day in and day out meant that he either believed me or didn't want to deal with me in full-blown hysterics again.

I appreciated his efforts, and we were getting along, united in our efforts to get out of the ranch. We looked forward to living in an apartment complex where we had no responsibilities for maintaining the property, and my ex could walk to the University.

My ex had started to tutor young students to make extra money. Two wealthy families in Cincinnati hired him. He would go to his client's home right after classes, and he started to return to the ranch later and later each night. One of the family's homes had a tennis court, and my ex, an avid tennis player, would stay at the client's home for dinner and play a few rounds of tennis before returning to the ranch.

Summer had started, and we were spending little time together. The realtor had shown the property to a few prospective buyers who were willing to buy it for way less than the reasonable asking price we had set for the property to sell it as soon as possible.

I started to protest against the late nights my ex was returning home. My ex would shrug his shoulders and tell me to find a "hobby." I would ignore his rudeness in response to my request to be brought along.

One weekend he did bring me along as the student's parents had invited us to a barbecue followed by a tennis match.

The student's parents greeted us at the door of the beautiful mansion. My ex's student stood at the door, a tall and gangly twelve-year-old boy who looked at us unsmiling with eyes filled with boredom. The stay-at-home mother greeted us with a big smile.

She wore an extremely short tennis skirt that exposed her long, bronzed legs.

The short-sleeved pink polo shirt showed her toned arms, She evidently never missed an opportunity to go to the gym.

The pink ankle socks and white tennis shoes completed the outfit. The woman's husband, a practicing psychiatrist, sat in silence in the living room, ignoring his guests and family as he read a book and puffed on a cigar.

My ex and the student's mother started talking immediately and never stopped; their attention focused on each other.

We ate dinner on the terrace overlooking the swimming pool and tennis court. The mother served the dinner, bringing platters of barbecue meats, corn, and baked potato to the table, excusing herself every time her breasts rested on my ex's back as she leaned forward over my ex to set the platters on the table.

The woman's husband was occupying the seat at the head of the table. He had brought the book he was reading and ate his dinner silently, turning the pages with his greasy fingers.

The twelve-year-old gobbled up his dinner, never lifting his face from the plate. He got up, walking to the pool area, where he sat at the edge, dangling his feet in the pool. The child had been largely ignored by his parents, who were both occupied with their objects of interest.

I ate my dinner in silence, observing the strange dynamic at the table. Soon we were all done with dinner, and my ex turned to me and said, "I know you don't play tennis; stay here while I play a few sets with her," pointing his finger at the student's mother in a playful manner.

They walked down to the tennis court together before I could respond. I would have tried my hand at tennis, but instead, I remained on the terrace, accompanied by the taciturn husband and his son, who was back from the pool and now read from a pile of cartoon magazines.

I looked at my ex and his tennis partner as they started to

play the first match. I could hear them laughing at missed balls; they would meet at the net after each game, and my ex would put his arm around her shoulders as they walked together to sit at the bench where they shared a small towel and drank water taken from a small fridge on the corner.

There was an aura of intimacy in their exchanges; I looked at the woman's husband to see if he noticed the flirtatious exchange going on under our noses.

Her husband had dozed off, holding the extinguished cigar between his fingers. I looked back at my ex, noticing his exaggerated serve and the forceful "ugh" he screamed every time he hit the ball.

I stayed seated until they finished their third match. I was alone on the terrace; the woman's husband and son had gone inside the house.

My ex walked back to the terrace slowly, his tennis racket resting on his shoulder, his other arm around the woman's shoulders, their heads bowed down as they spoke quietly.

My ex zipped the cover on the tennis racket and returned it to his student's mother as they exchanged a smile. My ex asked me, "Are you ready to go"? which I thought was a ridiculous question since I had been sitting alone, doing nothing the entire time, like a garden ornament. I stood up, extending my hand to our hostess without giving her any sign that would betray my feelings.

I thanked her for the lovely dinner and looked around to see if her husband had joined her. He hadn't; she walked us to our parked car, leaning on the opened driver's side window as she said goodbye to my ex and me. I waved goodbye feeling a mix of relief and apprehension.

I was glad I didn't have to watch my ex's flirtatious behavior that afternoon, and I was apprehensive because he knew that I knew. Perhaps nothing was going on between my ex and his student's mother; however, their body language said otherwise.

Their exchange denoted intimacy in each gesture as they word-lessly communicated desire and affection.

I leaned back as my ex backed the car out of the driveway. I thought about our first date, where I had witnessed his roving eye toward other women. He seemed to be seeking an acknowl-edgment of his desirability from each woman he stared at, the behavior deeply ingrained in his character.

I remembered my mother's reaction to my suggestion that the suitor she had chosen for me was a womanizer.

"Preposterous suggestion," she had said, reminding me of his position as a clergyman at our congregation.

A recalled few weeks after our wedding, my ex and I accom-panied my parents to a speaking engagement at our congrega-tion. A blond, young, and beautiful woman spoke about her experience as a journalist in a women's shelter in the Middle East.

There was a cocktail reception afterward. My ex accompanied me to our table and told me he would be coming right back.

I greeted friends who stopped by our table and decided to walk around and mingle after a while. I was comfortable social-izing without my ex, as I had always been in my previous rela-tionships.

I chatted with friends and my parents and saw my ex walking towards us. I reached for his hand, welcoming him with a smile.

My ex held my hand briefly, and then he asked my parents if they could give me a ride home.

I asked him, "Why?" He took me aside, away from my parents, and told me that he had invited the woman speaker to go out for a drink so that they could talk about the topic of that night's speaking engagement "in private."

I asked him if I could come; I had found the journalist's account of her experiences exciting and insightful…and I felt a bit jealous.

My ex looked at me with a haughty demeanor, which he

often used to discourage anyone who challenged his will. He answered, "No, you cannot come; the talk will be between two professionals; go wait for me at home." He turned around and left to meet the guest speaker. I returned to where my parents stood, obediently waiting to drive me home.

My mother looked at me, waiting for the explanation for my ex's sudden departure, leaving me there. My mom asked, "Where did he go?" I told her my ex's reason for needing me to get a ride home.

I studied my mother's face looking for any sign of disapproval.

She turned to my father and spoke to him in Polish, the language they used to communicate privately. My father looked at me; he embraced me, took me by the hand just like he did when I was little, and walked me to their car. I felt my father's reassuring grip, my mother reached for my other hand, and we walked to the car.

They drove me to my apartment in silence; I lived far from them, and my ex's request had been an imposition on my aging parents, but they did not complain. I waved them goodbye, and they drove home on a 40-minute ride.

I walked to the elevator and into our empty apartment on the 27th floor. I took a shower and selected the most charming outfit I could find. I stood in front of the mirror, looking at myself with a critical eye, ready to point out the deficits that had caused my ex's rejection.

That night was the start of the marriage dynamic, where I was eternally looking to catch up to my ex's standards and expectations. I would use humor to deflect the pain I felt with each insensitive remark he made about my inferior status.

I refused to listen to the internal voice that would point out the unfairness and cruelty of his remarks.

I had chosen him over the man whose heart I had broken, whose warm touch I craved, along with his reassuring embrace.

I knew I shouldn't think of anything other than making this

marriage successful. I looked at my ex's profile as he stared straight ahead, focusing on the road leading back to the ranch. I waited to devise a calm and reasonable way to address the evening's events at the Ohio mansion. I knew my ex would not respond well to arguments that would fail to articulate facts and supporting evidence.

I feared his ridicule; I continued to be more inclined to distrust myself. Years later, I understood that my self-mistrust was due to the first self-betrayal act as I walked away from my first experience of true love and connection.

I ignited my self-belittling by entertaining the thought that "my mind was playing tricks on me." We drove for at least twenty uncomfortable minutes when I decided to broach the subject.

"Your student lives in a very nice house." You can never go wrong by starting with a neutral statement, I told myself reassuringly; my ex answered "si" with a curt "yes" response.

"Did you enjoy the tennis match?" I tried again to engage him in conversation, and he answered, "Yes."

Now I was getting angry; how come he didn't ask if "I had a good time"? Or anything else, for that matter. I again broke the silence by commenting on his student's father, who had uttered two or three words maximum during the dinner. This time, there was no response.

The only thing left was to comment on the apparent flirtation between my ex and the student's mother.

I said, "I think you and your student's mother behaved inappropriately."

I immediately regretted my straightforward statement; I knew it sounded like an accusation, but I knew no other way to comment on his behavior and say it in any other way other than communicating my pain.

I said what I saw, and now I braced for his response.

My ex did not disappoint; he looked at me, eyes bulging in

anger; he called me by my first name, pronouncing each letter like he was hitting it with a hammer.

He told me that I "lacked sophistication and intelligence, as evidenced by my poorly articulated argument of a simpleton raised in a third-world country by superstitious parents from the Warsaw Ghetto."

My ex felt that his superiority over me extended to several factors, including his belief that Brazil, unlike Argentina, was a third-world country even though both were located in South America and equally mismanaged by a corrupt government.

The other factor he would bring up was my parents' background and lack of schooling and sophistication, as if they had a choice on the matter as they tried to survive the genocide that ended the lives of six million Jews.

His mention of the Warsaw Ghetto galled me. I could only imagine what my parents would say if they heard my ex's words of disdain for my parents' horrific experiences during the war.

I thought about the irony of my parents holding my ex in high regard, choosing him to be my husband and part of the family, begging me to "give him a chance" for their sake. I felt embarrassed for him and sad for us.

We arrived home, and my ex exited the car leaving me behind.

I got up and opened the front door whistling for Queenie, who came out excitedly. We walked outside in the dark.

That night I lost my fear that a Goblin or any such apparition would hurt me. I now realized that a human being could deliver real pain and anguish, and I finally admitted to myself that I was married to one such human.

I walked back to the ranch with Queenie following close behind me. I entered the dark living room where the atmosphere had always been heavy from day one, and now I felt the added layer of emptiness like I had entered into a vacuum.

My head was spinning with thoughts of wanting to run away

and never look back and the reality that there was nowhere to run.

My ex sat on the sofa watching TV. I could hear the laughter from the audience from our bedroom as I waited for my ex to come in for the nightly routine of carrying the mattress to the living room.

I got myself ready for bed and lay there, knowing there was no point in moving the mattress from the bedroom.

I arranged the pillows around my head, and I started to read from one of my favorite books, Jane Austen's *Pride and Prejudice.*

I imagined my ex morphing into a loving and devoted husband, just like Mr. Darcy, an arrogant and prejudiced man full of pride. I fell asleep in the bedroom, unperturbed by goblins, apparitions, or my ex, who had slept on the sofa in the living room.

In the morning, we received a call from the real estate broker, who informed us that he had a "serious" offer from a mobile home dealership owner interested in the 33 acres that came with the ranch. The good news got us talking again as I prepared breakfast in the kitchen. We drove to the realty office and signed the documents accepting the offer for the property in Loveland, Ohio.

My ex continued to tutor after attending his classes; he was close to completing his Master's degree as he had opted for the fast track, which meant longer hours in class and away from the ranch.

I packed our belongings and hired movers to take us to our new one-bedroom apartment in a complex near my ex's University.

My ex continued to come home late at night; I would close my eyes, pretending to be asleep. I had mastered the art of detachment that my ex seemed to prefer over my ebullient and emotional personality. I continued reading as many books as possible, and my English became fluent. Once back in Cincinnati, I worked as an assistant Kindergarten teacher in a large basement of a congregation.

The children were adorable, and I enjoyed the teacher.who weighed over 300 pounds, the children looked impossibly small around her, and I would join the kids watching her in awe as she sat her enormous backside on the tiny chairs balancing her body while an ukulele.

In the afternoons, I sat in front of a microfiche machine at my ex's college library, researching his thesis topic. We had reached some balance in our relationship that went on linearly, without many peaks or valleys.

My ex finished his classes and was now putting the last touches on his thesis due in a few weeks.

He had started interviewing prospective congregations looking for a religious leader. He had gone to Sydney, Australia, interviewing in a beautiful congregation near Elizabeth's Bay. My ex returned to Cincinnati and left again to interview in a small community in Holyoke, Massachusetts.

We were now waiting to hear from either place, my ex hoping to lead the thriving congregation in Australia.

I was also waiting... for my period to arrive. I stayed home one day feeling horribly nauseous and very tired.

I lay in bed with a cup of tea with Queenie as I calculate the dates on the "period calendar."

I told myself to stop relying on "denial" and accept that my period was very late. I called my ex to our bedroom, telling him about my symptoms and how late my period was.

His face turned pale, and he asked, "You think you are..." He apparently could not bring himself to finish the sentence. However, he agreed to go to the pharmacy and buy a pregnancy test.

My ex returned with five pregnancy tests of different brands recommended by the pharmacist.

I took all the tests, and all showed the same result. I was indeed pregnant. My ex's reaction to the news was hard to determine. His mind was impenetrable. His countenance didn't show joy or despair. At that point, I knew that my lonely childhood had uniquely prepared me to live with my ex.

I was amazed at the clever maneuvers of one wiggly bundle of cells and DNA that had managed to escape my ex's careful management of his life-giving equipment, finding a way to implant itself securely in my womb. "What a clever little being," I thought to myself, loving this child with every fiber of my being.

The pregnancy was confirmed by a doctor the same day we received the news that the Congregation in Sydney had decided to hire another candidate. My ex took the rejection badly; however, he had to go on and defend his thesis, successfully receiving his Master's degree in Religious Studies.

In the Fall of 1989, we returned to the car dealership where he had made our first American friend, the car salesman who unfortunately was not working there any longer. Another car salesman, equally enthusiastic as the former, sold us our new car.

We traded our blue Pontiac Grand Prix for a blue Jeep Grand Cherokee Wagoneer, a sturdy four-door SUV that we hoped would drive us safely in the streets of Holyoke, Massachusetts, where my ex had been hired as a leader for the close-knit community.

We left Cincinnati, Ohio, planning to make the fourteen-hour journey in two days. I sat in the passenger seat of our comfortable SUV, cradling Queenie and my growing belly simultaneously.

We were on our way to New England, where the Fall Season was legendary, with the tree leaves that changed into an array of colors ranging from yellow to bright red.

We looked forward to moving into the quaint blue Cape the Congregation provided to clergy as part of the package. We had seen pictures of the spacious interior and the small but charming backyard. The house was the last one tucked away in a dead-end street, ideal for our growing family.

Goodbye, Ohio; I said thank you for the lessons and the heartbreak that had taught us so much.

I was ready to start anew; with our child on the way, I hoped that my ex and I would grow closer, walking towards each other and breaching the divide that had kept us apart as we welcomed our child and stood together, side by side, looking at our new beginning.

**The end...for now**

# About the Author

To learn more about CeCe Rubin and discover more Next Chapter authors, visit our website at www.nextchapter.pub.

Frozen Brazilian Delight
ISBN: 978-4-82417-884-8

Published by
Next Chapter
2-5-6 SANNO
SANNO BRIDGE
143-0023 Ota-Ku, Tokyo
+818035793528

22nd April 2023

www.ingramcontent.com/pod-product-compliance
Lightning Source LLC
LaVergne TN
LVHW091433190726
843491LV00007B/1701